DRUG RUNNERS!

'Where's the stuff now? Did you at least get the coke?'

'Powell has it safe.'

'Did they have any more?'

Thomas shrugged. 'We didn't have time to check.'

'Well we can't risk it. We've already stirred up a hornet's nest. The police. Customs and Excise. Sooner or later they'll track down those kids, then Powell, then us. They'll have to go. They'll have to be taken care of, and fast. And no mistakes . . . no more bloody mistakes!'

Also by Ken Blake in Sphere Books:

THE PROFESSIONALS:
Operation Susie
KEN BLAKE

Based on the original screenplay by
Ranald Graham

SPHERE BOOKS LIMITED
30/32 Gray's Inn Road, London WC1X 8JL

First published in Great Britain by
Sphere Books Ltd 1982
Novelisation copyright © Sphere Books 1982

Set in Plantin

Printed and bound in Great Britain by
Hunt Barnard Printing Ltd., Aylesbury, Bucks.

Chapter One

Everything was too quiet; far too still. And as George Cowley allowed that nervous thought to run through his mind, he was not referring to the peaceful woodlands through which he was strolling.

He could just make out the house through the trees, a tall, Georgian mansion, partially screened by several massive and ancient yews along the edge of the lawns. The grounds of Reddington House covered one hundred and thirty acres, most of which had been left to develop into the sort of dry, attractive woodland through which Cowley was walking. An abode of many forms of wild-life, Cowley was more aware of a taller, darker life-form that seemed to stay half-hidden behind the trees: security men, and the sombre-faced bodyguards of the youthful Saudi prince to whom Reddington house was just one more 'holiday home'.

Prince Kefiri Hatak was walking beside Cowley, his hands clasped behind his back. His white suit was in brilliant contrast to his handsome, dark features; he was not happy.

'But I had been given to understand, Mr Cowley, that it was you yourself that established CI5 ...'

Cowley adjusted his jacket, slung across his arm, feeling slightly uncomfortable in the heat and extremely anxious to terminate this pointless interview as soon as possible.

'That is certainly true, Prince Hatak. But CI5 is an organisation established to fight domestic crime, whether home produced or imported. The men in its ranks are professionals of a very different calibre from your ordinary policeman, or military man. But they've all been recruited from the services. We fight crime with the same weapons that crime uses, with the same techniques.'

'I understand that perfectly well,' said Hatak, and insisted, 'which is why I can't understand your reasons for refusing your help to me.'

Cowley smiled as pleasantly as possible, his craggy features glistening slightly as perspiration – the result of sun and frustration – began to bead his skin. 'But Prince Hatak, no crime has been committed. My men are not –' he had been about to say 'babysitters' and caught himself in the nick of time. International incidents had been provoked by lesser insults. 'My men are not guardians, not bodyguards. It's true that at times they've functioned as such. But CI5 is the Action Squad. We rarely come into operation, invited to do so by one or other Ministry Department, until there is at least the *smell* of a crime.'

The hair on his neck bristled, an uncomfortable, slightly unnerving sensation. For over three weeks London had been dead. Nothing had happened at all, save for routine actions, and some dull surveillance operations. It was – Cowley was forced to admit – rather like the calm before the storm. He had an acute sixth sense for trouble, and trouble was looming.

It was far too quiet. Something would have to give ...

Cowley said, 'I'm sure that you'll find the boys from Special Branch quite excellently trained for the protection you require.' He stopped, turned to face Prince Hatak and began to shrug on his jacket.

Hatak shook his head, irritable, ready to object further. But from the direction of the house came a shout, the voice carrying weakly on the still summer air. Cowley turned to peer through the trees and his heart missed a beat. The call was for him, he just knew it. There was a man, standing at the edge of the lawns, waving his hand and shouting. The name he was shouting was Cowley's, and there was an edge of urgency in the way he beckoned.

At last!

Cowley excused himself and made his way briskly from the woodland, across the landscaped gardens and the beautifully maintained lawns, and into the house.

A man-servant held the phone out for him, then

discreetly retired. Cowley spoke quickly into the receiver, then said, 'Good God ... when?'

Moments later he was practically running from the house to his limousine, parked on the gravel driveway. It was an hour to London.

The storm was about to break.

Ray Doyle crouched at the end of the street, heart racing, breathing slightly laboured, his shock of dark, curly hair matted with sweat. He dragged a hand across his face, eyes alert for the slightest movements. His .44 magnum was a heavy, familiar and distinctly comfortable pressure against his left shoulder.

The street was still, deserted. It was an overcast day and the shop-windows were dull, lifeless; a stiff breeze cooled him, and he welcomed it. He was getting tired. The running was wearing him down. The pain in his chest was acute, the stitches long since out, but the scars of the gunshot wounds still red, still sensitive.

He decided to go. He rose from the crouch and stepped out into the street, walking slowly between the shops, alert for movement. The wind whipped up the dust and he blinked as his eyes stang for a second.

And in that second he glimpsed motion to his right!

The man had appeared in the window of the Iron-monger's. Doyle threw himself to the side, whipped out his pistol and pumped two quick shots into the man's chest. He was only half aware of the arm band, the black cloth tied around the man's arm, the sign of the enemy.

The window of the Ironmonger's shattered spectacularly and the man vanished from view, knocked backwards by the powerful .44 calibre slugs. Quickly Doyle climbed to his feet, slightly stooped, checking the street around him.

Movement from an alleyway!

Two handed, he raised the pistol, finger tightening on the trigger. A split second before he would have loosed the shot he realised that this was an innocent passer-by, someone puzzled by the sound of shooting and too stupid to stay back.

Doyle grinned, shaking his head at the narrow escape. He took four more steps forward ...

A window shattered behind him! He whipped round, shooting on the turn. The man was leaning out of the grocer's, and three spurts of dust before Doyle, and the accompanying roar of the automatic, were all Doyle needed to know before he shot back. The figure vanished, cleanly shot through head and heart.

Doyle grinned, raised his pistol as he backed on down the street. His left shoulder was throbbing, but his arm was as fast as ever. It was a month since he had ended his convalescence, after being shot three times by a terrorist, but already he could feel his reflexes returning to normal.

It was a good feeling too. The only irritation was that he couldn't run without getting breathless and breaking into a hard sweat. He had missed his squash practice, and it was a hard lesson to him that, though he was still in his twenties, it only took three months out of action for his body to get out of trim.

A voice spoke to him from the air. 'Stop looking so smug, Doyle. Check your right thigh.'

Doyle closed his eyes and swore, let the pistol arm drop as he stood in the street and checked his leg. A small red blob had adhered to his slacks, just above the knee.

'Damn ...'

In a real exchange of fire he would have been taken out totally by a wound like that. A second too slow; a moment's lakc of concentration. The split second of judgement that marked the difference between the soldier and the true professional.

'I'll get it back,' Doyle breathed, angry with himself, yet still conscious that he was not fully recovered from the assassination attempt upon him last Spring.

He had nearly died, and he had nearly died because he had been incautious, leaving his alarm lock disconnected while he had gone out for some shopping. She had been waiting for him in the shadows, pumping three shots through the carrier bag of supplies he had been clutching to his chest, blowing him backwards ...

4

He should have died. He would have died there and then if she had finished the job, but the girl's nerve had gone. She had left him for dead, not realising that one thing Ray Doyle possessed in abundance was the luck of the devil!

'Give it a rest, Doyle.'

The voice of the training monitor snapped Doyle's attention back to the artificial street, with its combination of enemy and friendly figures.

'Yeah. Put the kettle on.'

He walked slowly between the hardboard façades of the street, to the low, wide building behind, where the various offence capabilities of this Ministry training ground were controlled. He had done well, certainly. He had done very well indeed for a man who had had two slugs removed from his chest just three months before. But he had not done well enough.

That last one percent, as Cowley would say. He had still to pick up that vital, last one percent.

As he stepped into the monitor room, a phone was ringing. He reached for a cup of coffee, handed to him by a youthful, smiling man wearing a white laboratory coat, and sipped it gratefully.

'It's for you, Doyle. Cowley.'

Cowley? Calling him here? Doyle placed the coffee cup down and walked quickly across the room, eagerly snatching the phone from the man who held it towards him. What could Cowley possibly want with him now? Only last week he had been told, 'Another month at least, Ray. You're no good to me as you are. But I'm no fool, and I know how good you'll be in a month's time. Train. Get fit. Find the edge again.'

'Doyle here.'

Cowley's voice was hard, succinct. 'Get back to London. Now.'

'I was just shot in the thigh, sir. I feel you should know that.' He ran a hand through his tousled hair, half nervous of hearing the words from George Cowley that he so desperately wanted to hear.

'Be more careful,' Cowley said crisply. 'But as of now

5

you're back in action. We've got a D-One possible, and it looks big.'

A D-One! Drugs, drug trafficking ... but a D-*One*. The big haul. A potential trade in excess of a million pounds. Now Doyle understood why he was back on the roster.

'You and Bodie have handled a D-One before. It may be a false alarm, but we can't take that chance. Get back to London.' A pause, a brief hesitation, then the typical Cowley afterthought: 'You can return to training when this affair is blown over ...'

With a last burst of energy, Bodie raced to the top of the stairs and unlocked the door to his apartment, standing back to allow agent Five-two, otherwise known as Anne Page, into the bright, airy rooms.

Bodie was still dressed in his squash gear, his jumper round his neck, his lean, hard body looking good in white shorts and sweat-shirt. 'Enter,' he said to Anne, and she threw him a cool look, well aware that she was very much the fly entering the spider's parlour.

She was tall, blonde, and by Bodie's estimation, very beautiful. Since she had joined the ranks of CI5, just four months before, Bodie had been keenly eyeing her, and had had a free field ... since Doyle had been incapacitated after the attempt on his life.

'A shower first?' suggested Bodie. 'Or lunch?'

'Lunch, I think,' said Anne, throwing her racquet onto the settee and flopping down next to it. She looked around the elegantly furnished apartment, clearly impressed by Bodie's choice of prints, and by the shelf of sporting trophies. 'And after lunch *I'll* have a shower. And then *you* can have a shower.'

Bodie glanced at her from the kitchen, where he was checking the state of the lasagne he'd prepared that morning.

A day off. And a nice, bright, hot day at that. A day to woo and win the delicious Anne, with his exquisite squash playing, his elegant and witty banter, his supreme lasagne

. . . and his shower big enough for two athletic types to fit in together.

Anne said, 'Quite the sportsman, I see.'

'Good on the long jump,' he called back, and was pleased to hear her respond with a light laugh.

'How about the marathon?' she said. 'Or are you better at the sprint?'

Bodie brought through the dish of pasta and placed it on the table. 'Any distance that suits the occasion,' he said, and her eyes twinkled both with amusement and interest. Bodie straightened up, pleased with himself, feeling that the afternoon had almost been won (whether by himself or by Anne didn't matter to him; the result would be the same).

And of course, the telephone rang.

Anne Page laughed as she watched Bodie's face cloud over with irritation. 'That'll be George Cowley,' she said. 'I know his ring.'

'Nonsense,' Bodie said. 'It's the local Chinese take-away ringing to tell me about their new line in sweet and sour brawn.'

'It's George Cowley. Wants you on the job.' She smiled mischievously. 'Not quite the job you had in mind.'

'Definitely not.' Bodie hovered by the phone. 'It's Ray Doyle. Wants to have a drink tonight. Sorry Ray . . .'

'Answer the phone,' she said. 'Speak to George.'

'My mother,' Bodie surmised. 'Yes, she's about due for a call.'

He snatched up the phone. 'Hello, Mother. How's things?'

'Don't be funny, Bodie,' said George Cowley sharply from the other end.

'Hello sir,' said Bodie, deflated. Anne Page giggled silently, shaking her head as she watched the agony in Bodie's face.

Cowley said, 'We've got a possible D-One. Doyle's back on Operations, and I want you at H.Q. immediately. I know it's your day off, but I don't suppose you had anything planned.'

7

'That's true, sir,' said Bodie, looking at the lean and lovely legs of agent Five-two. 'I was just going to lay around all day.'

Cowley made a grunting sound at the far end of the line. 'I see. Well, I'm sorry, Bodie. You'll just have to make a date for another day.'

Chapter Two

The car turned into Westbury Grove, slowed for a moment, then accelerated down the street, finally to stop outside one of the tall, detached, Edwardian houses at the end of the row. It was a sleek, red Mustang, and it contrasted strongly with the rows of battered, patched and gaudily painted cars that lined both sides of the Grove.

Westbury Grove was one of those parts of North London that is destined to become fashionable, but for the moment, at least, has been allowed to become run down and practically totally turned over to students and single persons of foreign descent, desperate for cheap accommodation and needing easy access to the business parts of the city. The houses were badly in need of painting, the gardens overgrown, many of them filled with the remnants of cars that had been cannibalised for parts.

Dustbins and black rubbish bags abounded; in the hot summer afternoon the smell was offensively strong. Even the lime trees that were regularly placed along the street seemed to wilt with the heat and the smell, their branches drooping, their leaves a peculiar shade of yellow-green, unhealthy, dying.

The man who climbed out of the driver's seat of the Mustang was in his forties, a thick-set man wearing an impeccable Savile Row suit. He wore dark glasses, through which he peered with some disgust at the dilapidated neighbourhood as he buttoned up his jacket. His face was hard, a face lined with age and experience. The set of his mouth was that of a man with no sense of humour: grim, rather tight, exceedingly unfriendly.

His name was Charlie Powell. He was here to do business.

'Jesus, what a dump,' he said to the girl who climbed from the passenger seat.

9

'It's out of the way. It's ideal. The smell of rubbish doesn't affect the quality of the goods, Mr Powell.'

The girl was Diana Molner. Powell liked her hardness, the brazen way she answered back. She had the hint of a foreign accent – German, he thought. He liked a lot of things about her, not the least of which was her body. She was quite tall – in fact, she was an inch or two taller than Powell himself – and slim in all the right places, whilst filling her blouse quite adequately.

Powell was not a man of culture, nor of refinement. He had stared pointedly at Diana's body for most of the trip to Westbury Grove. He had even, at one point, allowed his hand to rest upon her slim knee, during a gear change, and had been disconcerted by the fact that she had made not the slightest move to remove it, nor had looked at him, nor commented.

Cool, he'd thought. Deliciously cool. Cool in company, an animal between the sheets.

Shame I've got to do what I've got to do . . .

If Powell was experiencing a certain sexual resonance with regard to Diana Molner, the reverse could not be said to be the case.

Diana found Charlie Powell one of the most repulsive men she had ever met. He smelled of sweat, mixed with cheap male deodorant spray. He licked his lips all the time. He was every bit the dirty, middle-aged man that Diana had grown up abhoring. He was almost certainly into pornography. It it wasn't for the fact that he also dealt in drugs she would have slapped his face and run a mile.

To get his money, she would suffer quite a lot.

Diana Molner was twenty years old, although some thought she looked more than that. If she was beautiful, it was a hard-edged beauty. Her eyes, bright and wide and very, very green, could narrow like an animal's. They were the eyes of a woman who has seen too much, and reacted too coldly to violence, to ever again be truly warm. Her blonde hair was long, well styled, something she allowed herself to indulge in, despite her loathing for all such self-obsessional trappings of the Imperialist society that, for the moment, was sheltering her.

'Follow me,' she said to Powell, and walked elegantly, and easily past him, through the broken gate at the end of one of the more overgrown gardens. She glanced up at the top floor as she walked, but saw no sign of movement. She walked up the crumbling concrete steps and rang on the entry phone.

Powell watched her easily as she bent to the grille and announced herself. A man's voice said, 'Okay,' and a low buzzing sound told of the front door being unlocked.

As Diana Molner led the way inside, Powell glanced back at the street. A black Rover had just pulled up, forty yards up the road. Two impassive faces watched the house, and Powell's entry.

They trotted quickly up the stairs, and at the top found the door to the flat held open by a thin young man wearing silver-rimmed spectacles. He peered intensely at Powell, before nodding almost cursorily.

'This is my partner,' she said. 'You can call him Philip.' She saw no reason to advertise his last name, Latimer.

Powell gave the youth a quick smile, noticing that Philip was nervous, wiping his hands on his faded denims. He smelled vaguely of dope. Powell thought that was funny, considering what he'd come here to take.

He walked into the large, untidy room. It was a typical student's room, sparsely furnished, with more attention being paid to the posters that covered the walls than to the comfort of the seating. The posters were mostly music advertisements, the inevitable Jane Fonda, seated cross-legged on the beach, and several Chinese prints. On the bare table were scattered dirty plates and cutlery, a half eaten loaf, and a bottle of creamy milk.

'Nice place you've got here,' said Powell, with as much heavy sarcasm as he could manage. Philip just smiled. Diana Molner walked into the bedroom and reappeared a moment later with a small, black suitcase.

She was followed from the room by a good-looking teenaged boy, who eyed Powell suspiciously. The boy was blond, well tanned, lean of hip and chest. He wore a tight, white T-shirt and tight, fashionable jeans. He kept his back against the wall all the time.

He was introduced as Rudi. Powell had already guessed that this was Rudiger Molner, Diana's younger brother.

'All right, let's see it,' Powell said abruptly.

Diana had placed the case on a cleared area of the table, and she snapped the locks open to display the contents.

Powell walked over to the table and peered down at the array of fifteen or so polythene bags, with their powdery white content. He glanced at Diana and smiled, then reached down and shuffled the bags around.

'They say clever people can predict which bag will be tested. So I always like to randomise the process.'

When he was satisfied that any cunning lay-out, designed to make him test the one or two bags of the real thing among a greater content of some cheaper drug had been disrupted, he pinched open one of the polythene sacks, dipped his finger and thumb into the powder and felt it, rubbing it slowly between the skin surfaces.

'*Feels* like the real thing,' he said easily, letting the caution in his voice sound almost like sarcasm.

Rudiger Molner, seated on the windowsill, quietly watching, let a thin, contemptuous smile touch his lips. Diana Molner and Philip Latimer just stood and watched as Powell examined the merchandise. They looked anxious, uncertain. They were less than the full professionals they had played up to being.

Powell took out a small piece of tin foil from his wallet, flattened it on the table and pinched a small amount of the white powder into a pile in the middle. Holding it up, he heated it from below using his elegant gold cigarette lighter.

The powder melted and bubbled, and he watched it, inwardly impressed at the quality, mentally calculating just how much of the stuff the kids were in possession of.

The youth called Philip said, 'It's good stuff. There's no speed in it.'

Powell didn't need to be told. It was all he could do to

12

keep his excitement from registering.

He glanced at the case, at the bulging polythene sacks of what he was fast coming to believe was the highest quality cocaine that he'd ever come across.

Cocaine! Eight or ten kilos of the stuff!

Where in the name of God had these fresh-faced kids come up with such a quantity of one of the world's most popular drugs? The street price alone ... Powell couldn't imagine. For high grade cocaine, with its demand from the rich, trendy section of society, the price was formidably high!

He said to Diana Molner, 'How much are you asking?' As he spoke he placed the split sack back in the case and closed the lid.

The girl's hesitant answer told Powell everything he needed to know. He caught Diana's quick glance at the man called Philip. When she looked back at him she was hard again, sounding very positive. 'A hundred thousand. That's the price to you.'

Powell laughed. He snapped the locks on the case and shook his head. He'd already estimated the street value of the drug consignment at between two and three hundred thousand pounds, so the price she was quoting was unprofessionally high in any event.

He said, 'You must be kidding. A hundred thousand? Where have you been dealing before?'

Philip looked upset, confused. He said, 'Oh come on, there's ten kilograms there. That's a lot of coke. Our price is set – a hundred thousand.'

'Far too high,' said Powell, coldly.

Diana looked more than a little flustered. It had all worked so smoothly up until now, and now, at the moment which was crucial to both sides, they were up against a cool, hard professional, who clearly wasn't going to play their game.

She sounded almost as if she were pleading as she said, 'Ten kilograms! That'll fetch a quarter of a million! Two hundred and fifty thousand quid!'

'Perhaps a little higher,' Powell agreed. 'The street price varies. It's good at the moment. Good from the point of view of people like me.'

'Well then!'

Powell smiled at her. He had also noticed that Rudiger had straightened slightly, propped up against the window-ledge; his hands looked stiff, held by his sides.

Shit! The kid's got a gun.

Powell said, 'I'll think about it.' He picked up the case and took a step backwards. Diana stared at him blankly for a second, then realised what he was about to do. Philip frowned, then opened his mouth to object.

Rudiger stepped across the room quickly, his slim body moving lithely, threateningly. 'Put that down,' he said. His pale eyes shone with anger. He reached for the case that Powell held.

Powell placed a brawny hand on the boy's chest and pushed him away. Rudi lurched backwards against the table. Powell shouted, 'Stay back, kid! If you don't want to get hurt! Stay back.'

'No way!' shouted Rudi.

Philip said, 'That's our property! Put it down.'

'You're out of your depth, kid. Stay out of it. Count yourself lucky.'

'No!' screamed Philip, and stepped forward angrily.

The door was suddenly kicked open and two men ran into the room; they were both middle-aged, wearing dark glasses and dark suits, and they stood just inside the room, staring at the three kids, smiling. One of them said, 'Having a little trouble with the children, Powell?'

'I don't think so,' Powell said. 'They don't like having their toys stolen, but I expect they'll get some more.' He began to back towards the door and his two colleagues.

And then it happened.

Rudiger reached quickly behind his back and tugged a small-calibre pistol from his belt. He raised it, two handed, pointed squarely at Powell.

'Drop the case!' he shouted. 'Drop it! Now!'

'Don't be stupid, kid,' said Powell grimly.

Diana was horrified to see her brother threatening such violent action. From the look of shock on her face she hadn't even known that Rudi was in possession of a gun. She shook her head, a silent plea, then found the voice to cry, 'Rudi! No ... not that way!'

Rudiger Molner threw her an angry, almost desperate glance. He looked, suddenly, very vulnerable, standing in the middle of the room, slightly stooped, the gun shaking in his two-fisted grip.

'Get back!' he snapped at Diana, and she obeyed quickly, Philip too, the two of them pushing themselves back against the wall.

Powell and the other two stood beside the door, stiffly, attentively, wearing Rudiger down with the implacability of their stare.

'Drop the case,' Rudi said, but Powell just shook his head.

'You won't fire that gun. You've lost, kid. Be a good boy and give it up.'

'*Drop the case!*'

'Drop dead,' said Powell, and laughed.

Rudiger Molner's face suddenly drained of all colour. Powell knew the signs, and even as the boy fired the gun, Powell was moving, flinging himself to one side, taking routine evasive action.

His two companions did the same.

The shot had been intended to miss. It smashed into the plaster above the door, sending a great cloud of white dust drifting to the floor. The noise was deafening, and Diana screamed loudly, more from the sudden shock than from any feeling that her brother had killed one of the men.

Rudiger still stood, shaking like a leaf, the gun wavering as he held it, pointed towards the door. Everything was happening too fast. He was vaguely aware that one of the strangers, rolling across the floor, was tugging a gun from the inside of his jacket.

'Hey, what's going on?' came a woman's voice from the landing, and the door, swinging free, was pushed open.

'Pamela ... get back!' yelled Philip.

'Pamela!' screamed Diana Molner.

She stood in the doorway, a plump, attractive girl in her late teens. She wore typical student's clothes, faded jeans and a baggy, kaftan-type blouse. Her hair was tied back from her face, her eyes peering widely, astonishedly, from behind gold-framed glasses.

She had been trying to study next door, and the sudden racket had disturbed her, made her worried.

She had come in to find out what was going on, and to ask her neighbours to keep their voices down. The sudden shot had startled her.

But still she stepped into the room.

'*Pamela!*'

Diana's scream of warning distracted the man on the floor who held the gun. He had been about to shoot at Rudi. Now he twisted round and pumped two quick shots into the girl who suddenly loomed above him.

The rounds were forty-four calibre. The range was six feet. The girl was lifted into the air, arms flailing, face a rigid mask of shock, chest blossoming into the cruellest red rose. She struck the wall of the landing, and tumbled in a ragged heap to the ground, her face still turned towards the room, eyes watching almost curiously as death drained their sparkle.

Rudiger shot again, the bullet smashing into the floorboards beside Powell's scrabbling body. The man had jumped to his feet, grabbed for the case, and was running to the door. The man with the gun twisted round and shot back at Rudiger. The shot went wild. His second shot struck Philip in the chest as Philip raced for cover.

Diana just stood, silently watching the mayhem, her hands clasped to her ears.

A moment later Powell and his two colleagues were gone. Rudiger was standing by the table, murmuring, 'Oh sweet Christ. Oh Christ, what have we done?'

Philip lay sprawled on the floor, mouth moving but emitting no sound. Diana went to him and knelt beside him, beginning to cry. She picked up his hand and kissed it, then cradled his head in her lap, rocking backwards and forwards. Philip began to shake, and his hands clutched at her, his eyes turned widely on her, desperately pleading for help as his life ebbed.

Rudiger came over and stared at his friend, then looked at Diana Molner helplessly.

'What are we going to do?' he said, and when his sister shook her head, he repeated, his eyes closed, 'Oh Christ, what are we going to do?'

Chapter Three

There were many things that Ray Doyle hated in life; he hated over-cooked meat and bad Chinese food; he loathed dizzy debutantes and T.V. police shows; he could be reduced to apoplectic rage when confronted with someone busy 'getting into their head', spouting a pseudo-Zen jargon and believing that 'everything in the world was okay if you believed it to be okay'.

But if there was one thing that Ray Doyle hated above all these things, it was drugs. He was not a prude, he just hated the waste that the drug market, and the drug culture represented.

He hated to see families struggling on the break-point because they couldn't support the habit of one or other of the parents.

He hated the abuse of money by a class with more money than respect for society, the rich kids, blowing more on an evening's cocaine than Doyle could earn in a week.

He hated what drugs did to people, the way people were changed by them, addictive or non-addictive both. Buzzed out on speed, an attractive girl was just as attractive, but there was no way of relating to her, no way to interact on a level deeper than physical gratification.

And Doyle couldn't stand that.

As he drove through North London an image was playing through his mind, an image nearly as powerful as that of the girl who had shot him, just three months before. It was a memory of a 'facing off', just himself and a thin, shaking youth, who waved a gleaming black magnum forty-four at him, and shrieked abuse.

Doyle knew how to cope with a straight confrontation. His police training had taught him how to remain cool; his Professionals' training had taught him how to read the signs, how to look for the colour change in the face, the whitening of the knuckles, the dilation of the eyes, the sudden dryness of the lips. He had been under fire, and under the threat of fire, very many times.

He was still alive to prove that he knew how to handle a situation like that.

But this kid had been wrecked on speed. He hadn't slept for days, that much was clear. The junk was practically coming out of his skin. He had bounced off the walls and the chairs, he was like a bee, buzzing about the room, a frantic, confused focus of energy, of alertness, of panic and lost control.

The gun had waved this way and that. The kid had screamed at Doyle, then laughed, then almost cried. He could hardly focus on the CI5 man, and his gaze flittered restlessly about the room.

And Doyle had not known how to read the situation, how to gauge the tightening of the finger on the trigger, how to tell whether the speed-freak would lose total control and just start to fire wildly.

For the first time in a long time, Doyle's nerve had gone; the kid was buried in Harrow cemetery; the incident remained to haunt Doyle too often for his liking.

So on his way to Westbury Grove he felt cold, angry. A kid had died, so Control had informed him.

He had been driving up from the west, thinking to meet Cowley at H.Q., but the D-One had blown wide open while he had still been on the motorway, and he was to meet Cowley and Bodie at the scene.

A kid was dead. A girl.

And it looked for all the world as if she had just got into the line of fire.

Drugs! And kids with the romantic notion that to saturate their skulls with consciousness-expanding junk was somehow adult, was a maturing thing to do, was a way of increasing experience. If only they could see themselves, sitting around like zombies, talking crap, denying reality . . .

As he arrived at the house, pulling into the side of the road between two patched up, gaudily painted pre-sixties

Hillmans, Cowley was just arriving too.

They trotted up the steps together, and Cowley glanced back at the dilapidated avenue, shaking his head. 'In five years time this will be the new Hampstead. Look at it now!

'Shall we get inside, sir?'

Cowley glanced at him sharply. 'This upsets you.' It was a statement, not a question. They walked up the stairs.

'Yes it does. Perhaps I shouldn't be assigned to the case.'

'Nothing of the sort,' said Cowley. He had taken off his jacket. It was hot in the house, and the smell of refuse was quite cloying. 'I need a man acting for me who cares a little for the consequences behind the crime.'

They arrived at the upper landing and were met by a police Inspector called Harrington. Cowley introduced himself, and Doyle, but Doyle had eyes only for the rug covered heap on the landing. He let his gaze drift from the great streak of blood down the wall, to the tips of the fingers of a hand, just poking out from below the rug. He knelt beside the body, tugged back the rug and stared, for a second, at the dull-eyed face that seemed to watch him. She had been very young. She had been pretty. The gold-rimmed glasses seemed incongruous upon her, now that she was dead.

'Nasty,' Doyle said, the only word he could find that didn't make him clench up inside.

'Where's the cocaine?' asked Cowley, and Harrington replied, 'In the cupboard, across the room.'

Doyle climbed to his feet and followed Cowley into the apartment. Bodie was there, standing by the window, staring around at the disorder and general untidyness of the room. He smiled at Doyle.

Seated at the table, smoking a cigarette nervously, was an Indian youth. He glanced anxiously at Cowley and Doyle as they cast quick, questioning looks at him. A uniformed policeman stood by.

'Who's that?' Cowley said softly to Harrington.

'Lives in the building. Name of Patel. Quite helpful, but terrified. Got a typical Asian's attitude to police, assumes we're going to crush his privates to get what we want out of him.'

Inside the cupboard lay the remnants of the operation, an operation – a deal – that had clearly gone badly wrong. Cowley picked up the small scales and the empty polythene bags. Propped up in a corner was a bag still filled with cocaine. Cowley picked it up and hefted it, then placed the scales back on a level surface and carefully weighed the sample.

'A pound,' he said thoughtfully. 'A good old standard pound weight of cocaine. That strikes me as an odd amount.'

'Struck us that way too, sir,' said Harrington.

There was a smear of powder on the cupboard shelf. Doyle touched his finger to it, then tasted the residue on his skin. He wiped it from his tongue almost immediately and shook his head. 'It's not castor sugar. If that stuff's pure, that bag alone is worth about twenty grand.'

'If it's really pure,' said Cowley quietly, 'It's worth nearer forty. The market is good at the moment ... but a pound, not half a kilogram ... that's odd.'

Bodie called to them. 'You might like to take a look over here, good buddies ...'

Doyle walked across to him and crouched where Bodie was indicating a blood stain on the wall, low down, well away from the hall. Cowley stood above them, solemnly thoughtful.

'Can't be hers,' Cowley said, nodding back towards the dead girl.

'Someone else must have got hurt,' said Doyle.

'Obviously,' said Bodie, and grinned. 'How's the training session? Got your wits back yet?'

Doyle just said, 'My wits, yes. My strength, yes. It's tolerance I'm still short on.'

Bodie got the hint.

Attention focused upon Sanjit Patel. As the three CI5 men gathered round him, he grew noticeably more edgy, drawing deeper on his cigarette, eyeing Bodie in particular, whom he seemed to regard as particularly threatening.

Cowley sat on the edge of the table, smiled at the young man, trying to put him at his ease. 'Do I understand that it was you who gave the alarm?'

'Yes sir. I called the police.'

He smoked quickly, then stubbed out the butt on one of the crumb covered plates left by the occupants of the flat.

'What's your name?'

'Patel. Sanjit Patel.'

'And where do you live, Sanjit?'

'One floor below. In fact, directly below this flat. I've lived here for four years.'

Doyle said, 'So you knew the people who lived here. In this flat?'

Patel stared at him, then gave a little shrug. 'He hadn't lived here that long. I saw him occasionally. He played his music very loud, and sometimes there were other sounds. But he kept to himself.'

'Sanjit ...' Cowley leaned forward, trying to be as friendly, as encouraging as possible. The Asian was shaken, that was clear enough, shaken by the death of the girl, and the battering of questions to which he had already been subjected by the police. 'Tell me what happened. Tell it again. Everything, everything you remember. Everything you heard.'

Patel fumbled in a pack of Embassy for another cigarette. 'I was working. Downstairs. I was reading a book, and I could tell there were several people up here because the floorboards were creaking. Like someone walking up and down. There were voices. They were waiting for someone. He paused to strike the cigarette, inhaled deeply, almost with relief.

'And then?' Cowley prompted.

Sanjit rubbed a thumb across his eyebrows. He looked weary. 'And then two people went up the stairs. For a while there was just the murmur of voices from up here, then there was the shot. At first I thought it was an explosion, like a gas stove. I jumped out of my skin. Then I realised that there was a lot of shouting, the voices very raised. Another shot,

22

and another. Then lots of feet on the stairs. I was frightened
...'

'So you stayed inside your own room,' suggested Bodie.

But Sanjit shook his head. 'No. I don't know why, but I
went out onto the stairs. A foolish thing to do, considering
what happened to ...' his voice thinned, and he cast an
agonised glance towards the landing.

Doyle, impatiently, said, 'You went to the stairs. And
then what? Who did you see?'

'They were dragging Philip out. He was hurt. Very badly,
I think.'

'Philip,' repeated Cowley. 'Which Philip would that be?'

'The man who lived here.'

'Who were dragging him?' asked Doyle. 'What did they
look like?'

'They were other students, I think,' murmured Patel.
'They were certainly young. I've seen them before, too.
They've visited quite a lot.'

'How many?' Cowley asked.

'Two. A boy and a girl. Very good looking, very blond.
They looked very alike, like brother and sister. Maybe they
were.'

Bodie said, 'Did they see you?'

Patel nodded, shivering at the recollection. 'Indeed yes.
The boy had a pistol. He was very angry, very frightened I
think. His chest was covered with blood, but it was Philip's
blood. He shouted at me to get back into my room, and I did.
Very fast. I was very frightened too.'

'And what did you do? They left the house. Did you
watch them go?'

Patel shook his head. 'I confess no. I listened until I heard
them go through the front door, then I went upstairs and
found ... and found Pamela ...' he started to shake,
frowning deeply, on the verge of tears, Cowley thought. 'It
was terrible. She was ... she was so nice ...'

Doyle said, 'How about other people in the building?
Where is everybody?'

Patel had slumped forward, head in his hands, the

cigarette smoking to extinction between his fingers. Quietly, he said, 'On vacation. Pamela and I were studying for an exam. A special exam ... she was helping me ...'

Doyle and Bodie exchanged a glance, Doyle questioning with the way he raised his eyebrows; Bodie thought for a second, then nodded. They were agreed. Pamela and Sanjit Patel had been a little closer than just fellow students. But Patel was not prepared to admit to that fact.

Cowley stood up from the table and walked across to the window, peering down into the debris-littered front garden. 'Did they have a car, Mr Patel? Did you see a car at all?'

Patel shook his head glumly. 'I didn't look out.'

'But you said you'd seen the other two before,' said Doyle. 'The blonds. Did they have a car then? It's important, Sanjit. Really important that you try to remember.'

'I just don't know. I'm sorry. I never took that much interest in them.'

Cowley turned from the window. 'And the man who owned this apartment, Philip –' he glanced at Inspector Harrington, 'Philip what? What was his other name?'

'Latimer, sir. Philip Latimer.'

'Philip Latimer,' Cowley repeated, filing the name. To Patel, 'What did he study? Any ideas?'

Patel swivelled slightly in his chair, searching back through brief, unsatisfactory conversations with his upstairs neighbour.

'He was doing research of some sort. Postgraduate research, I'm sure. He was quite bright. I think his field was biology, or biochemistry ... something like that. I'm not fully sure.'

'Thank you, Mr Patel. I think you can go.' Cowley smiled pleasantly. The Asian youth walked gratefully back to his own room, and Doyle joined Cowley by the window, watching as an ambulance arrived on the scene, siren sounding, blue-light flashing frantically. The ambulance men leapt from the cab and began to race towards the house, carrying a stretcher. A uniformed sergeant walked towards them, waving his hands: don't hurry, the girl's dead.

Cowley said, 'Well? What d'you think?'

Ray Doyle shrugged. 'Certainly doesn't sound like the Mafia.'

Bodie added, 'Unless they've started recruiting kids.'

Doyle said, 'But the Mafia don't usually leave twenty grands worth of dope behind. Seems a little careless –'

'A little amateur –'

'A little beginner's bad luck.'

Cowley said nothing, just listened. Bodie eventually asked, 'So what do we do? Follow it up? Or leave it to the drug squad?'

Cowley turned to face his two men, leaning against the windowsill, thoughtfully impassive. He slowly shook his head. 'We had a tip-off that a D-One was in the offing. Large haul of drugs, saturating the market. Odd thing . . . the tip-off seemed to come from a worried member of the syndicate. There's something not right, something that is very definitely as far away from being 'right' as possible. It's not organised crime, but it's too close for comfort. We stay with it.'

Doyle suggested, 'Gang warfare?'

'Maybe. But I don't like the sound of the kids involved. Hardly Triad members; hardly your street-wise Londoners.'

Something had occurred to Bodie. 'Marijuana started in the universities. Maybe someone's trying the same with cocaine?'

But Cowley shook his head. 'Cocaine's a rich man's drug. How many students could afford it? They'd go for speed. Wouldn't they? They'd have to.'

'But someone laid out for this little lot,' said Doyle. 'And there's cocaine powder on the table. That pound weight may not have been all that was here.'

'Maybe they stole it,' said Bodie. 'And the syndicate came and took it back. The hard way.'

Cowley nodded. 'Highly feasible.' He hefted the sack of cocaine, staring at it. 'Find out everything you can about this Latimer, also the dead girl. And see if you can get a useable description of the two that dragged Latimer away.'

He looked down at the cocaine. 'Three times the price of gold ...'

Bodie added, 'Three times as deadly.'

The gleaming grey Rover 2000 slid quietly to a stop at the side of the road, just before the arch of the railway bridge. The driver climbed easily from the car, locked the door and looked around.

He was middle-aged, tall and hard looking; his suit was that of a businessman, but his general demeanour was harder.

His name was Raoul Northcott.

He walked across the bridge, towards the red saloon car that was idling some way away. In the middle of the bridge he stopped and leaned on the dirty, grey iron of the walls, staring down at the complex of railway lines below, watching the sleek electric trains running north from King's Cross.

From the saloon, two men stepped towards him. Their names were Dan Harris and Joe Thomas. They wore dark glasses, and carried themselves with the awkwardness of men over-muscled, and overloaded with weaponry, for the smartly cut suits they wore.

The taller of the two, Thomas, had earlier that afternoon shot and killed a girl student called Pamela.

Northcott looked round at them as the three of them met together. He didn't smile as he straightened up. 'Well? How'd it go?'

Thomas smiled thinly, removing his sun-glasses and glancing at a noisy diesel locomotive passing below the bridge. 'We leaned on them.'

'I'm glad to hear it,' said Northcott.

'They shouldn't be any more bother.'

Northcott nodded. 'Well done. It's how I like a 'leaning' to go. Nice, clear communication between people. Communication is the key to a happy life ...' he grinned, but the smile faded from his face as he saw the solemn expressions of his two juniors. 'Oh yeah?' he said, nervously.

Harris said, 'It wasn't quite as easy as all that.'

Thomas added, 'We had a slight problem.'

'Wonderful,' said Northcott sourly. 'Bloody wonderful. I should have known better than to assume you two would carry anything off without cocking it up. What sort of problem?'

'An accident,' said Thomas.

Northcott sighed, shaking his head with irritation. 'An accident. So what sort of accident would that be, exactly?'

'Shooting,' said Harris.

And Northcott just closed his eyes, feeling cold, feeling irritable, feeling more than a little shocked. 'Oh my God,' he said.

'It was unavoidable,' explained Thomas. He glanced nervously at his partner. The bridge shook, slightly, as an Inter-City express thundered below them, heading out of London.

'How serious is it?' asked Northcott.

'Pretty serious.'

'What happened? Exactly! What made it happen?'

Harris said, 'They drew on us. We had no choice. We went into the flat, as planned, as back-up to Powell. The kids were shocked, taken by surprise, but one of them had a gun. He drew on us, and he looked crazy. Probably on a toke of the junk himself. He looked – really! – like he was going to shoot to kill.'

'We had no choice,' Thomas repeated.

'And you left what? What carnage?'

'One of them badly wounded,' Thomas said. 'Not the one with the gun, an older kid. Maybe mid-twenties. And a girl. She came in from behind, surprised us. She's, er ... well. She's dead for sure. Gut shot.'

Northcott exploded with anger, face reddening, fists clenching at his sides as he turned away from his two men, then leaned heavily on the side of the bridge. 'You bloody fools! For Christ's sake, they were just kids! You know what we agreed! Kids, young, harmless ...'

Thomas sniggered at the use of the word harmless. 'They were armed. It was them or us, what the hell were we supposed to do? It all happened very fast; you don't have time to think about shooting to disarm, or incapacitate. You shoot to save your life ... by killing.'

'All right, all right. Let's not go on about it.' Northcott remained silent for a moment, thinking hard. He glanced at Harris. 'Where's the stuff now? Did you at least get the coke?'

'Powell has it safe.'

'Did they have any more?'

Thomas shrugged. 'We didn't have time to check.'

'Of course not,' said Northcott sarcastically. 'Too busy shooting and running.' He paced away from the two men, hands in his pockets.

Finally he turned, came back to them and said, almost softly. 'Well, we can't risk it.'

'Can't risk what?'

'We've already stirred up a hornet's nest. The police. Customs and Excise. Sooner or later they'll track down those kids, then Powell, then us. They'll have to go.'

Thomas frowned as he said, 'Who, the kids?'

Northcott nodded. 'They'll have to be taken care of, and fast. And no mistakes ... no more bloody mistakes!'

He turned and walked briskly back to his car.

Thomas watched him go, then turned to follow Harris back to their own vehicle. 'I'm not happy about this,' he said softly. 'Not happy at all.'

Chapter Four

For Diana Molner, the real nightmare began about an hour after the shooting.

For an hour there had been no time to think straight about anything except the desperate need to escape from the area of Westbury Grove, to drive somewhere crowded, where they might lose themselves, and to get the minimal medical supplies possible to attend to Philip.

They carried Philip between them from the house, threatening the downstairs student, Patel, so loudly that they guessed they might have had a few minutes grace before he called the police.

Rudi's battered and time-scarred Renault was parked a hundred yards down the road, and that slow drag from house to vehicle seemed to drain all Diana's strength. She was sweating profusely when at last Rudi opened the rear door of the car and eased Philip's shaking, barely conscious body into the back seat. He covered the older youth with a smelly car rug, trying to keep the woollen surface from touching the raw wound in Philip's chest.

'Get in,' he snapped to Diana. She had tugged her coat on over her dress, to cover the splashes of blood on her waist. She gratefully climbed into the passenger seat and turned, to reach for Philip's icy hand.

'Quickly, Rudi. Quickly for God's sake.'

'Shut up!' her brother snapped. He started up the car. The Renault was eight years old, recently serviced, but its engine roared loudly; hardly the most discreet of machines. It lurched forward from the kerb, then picked up speed as Rudi span the wheel violently.

With a screech of suspension, they began the frantic drive west.

'Here. Stop here!'

They had been driving for thirty minutes, Rudi handling the car almost recklessly. His lean, youthful features were set grim and anxious, and Diana could see that his mind was as much on the fact that they had been ripped off as on the immediate problem of Philip Latimer. Sweat dripped from him; he changed gear too early, too late, used the brakes like a beginner. If loss of blood was threatening Philip's life, Rudi's driving was a danger too.

They were some miles from Westbury Grove, in an area of London that Diana didn't recognise. They had passed between a row of shops, and she'd seen a pharmacy. Rudi pulled into the kerb, and leaned back to tug the rug right over Philip's head while Diana ran across the road to buy the medical supplies they needed.

Her mind was whirling. She was no nurse, and had little idea what was available to help in such situations. She just knew that Philip was dying . . .

The sudden agony that surfaced, the sudden awesome sense of loss, made her go dizzy, become confused for a second as she entered the store. Tears stang her eyes, but she shook them away, and quickly prowled round the shelves.

She bought bandages, plasters, germoline and iodine. A box of tissues also seemed like a good idea, and a bottle of Perrier water. Cotton wool she added as an afterthought. At the counter she discovered that penicillin was only available on prescription, and she was too nervous of arousing suspicion to press her case. She was given an ointment for the 'deep cut' that she said her husband had inflicted upon himself in the garden.

Then she walked as steadily as possible back to the car, where brother Rudiger was waiting impatiently, in a frenzy of panic.

They drove on again, this time seeking a quiet area, where for a few minutes they might attend to Philip without fear of being observed. Rudi finally parked the car near to some waste ground, overlooking allotments. The nearest building was a block of flats, and although several children were playing football at the front of them, there was no one else about.

Diana knelt up on the passenger seat, and reached over to uncover Philip Latimer. He lay with his eyes closed, his mouth slightly open.

'He's not conscious any more,' said Diana, and felt her whole body go cold. She found herself willing him to live, desperate for him to live, and not to leave her, now. Philip had been the quietly strong one in the group, the real decision maker. In the time she had known him she had come to more than like him.

For a few weeks, despite the exhilaration and the obsession of all of them with their plan for selling cocaine, she had been in love with the young man who lay bleeding to death in the back seat.

Rudi said, 'Can you feel his pulse?'

Diana reached for Philip's hand and felt quickly for the pulse. She pressed and squeezed, thought she'd detected it, but then couldn't be sure. She touched his neck, looking for the jugular. The cold shock increased as she thought, *Oh God no, he's gone! He can't have gone* . . .

Then she felt the merest tremble of a beat, and as she kept her finger in position so she established that a faint, but quite rapid pulse, was beating through Philip's system.

Her own heart slowed, a feeling of relieved warmth coursed through her skin.

Quickly, then, she unscrewed the bottle of Perrier water, soaked a wad of cotton wool wrapped in gauze, and dabbed at the blood and ragged flesh on Philip's chest. The blood had largely congealed, but a thin trickle was still draining down into his clothes. He was such a mess that her efforts were almost pointless.

She soaked a tissue with water and dabbed at Philip's lips, willing him to respond with a murmur, with a flickering opening of his eyes.

Come back. Please, Phil. Come back to me . . .

The tears came, then, coursing down her cheeks as she dabbed and cleaned the gunshot wound. Rudi watched her, pale and cold, his eyes glittering and hard, more through fear than disapproval of his sister's grief.

Diana smeared antiseptic ointment on the torn flesh, then

31

as best she could she wrapped bandages around him, winding them as tight as possible. Within seconds they were blood saturated and useless and she sank back on her haunches in despair. The wound was potentially mortal. He needed surgery, and he needed surgery urgently.

'It's no good, Rudi. It's no good. I don't know what to do.' She became tearful, a touch angry. 'We have to take him to a hospital.'

Rudiger shook his head, looking instantly worried. 'We can't,' he said, and his voice was cold. 'We can't take the chance.'

'We *must* !' Diana screamed at him, and she cried a little more openly. 'Look at him! I can't stop the bleeding. He's bleeding inside as well, into his lungs! He must be! Rudi, for God's sake, we've *got* to get him medical attention!'

'Out of the question.'

'Rudi, I love him! I can't bear the thought of him dying. Rudi!'

Her brother reached an arm around her, compassionate for the first time in an hour. He let her cry against his shoulder, while he stared out across the waste ground, his face set grim, his mind a turmoil of confused thoughts and vague plans.

He said, 'The police will be watching the hospitals. They'll know that one of us is hurt, and they'll have every emergency ward under surveillance.'

Diana jerked back from him, wiping a hand across her eyes. 'It's a risk we have to take,' she said coldly.

Rudi shook his head. 'We don't dare.'

'Rudi! He's dying! If we don't act now he's got no chance. I don't want two deaths on my conscience.' She stared at Philip's wan, drawn features, feeling bitterly sad inside. 'I especially don't want him to die ...'

But Rudi reached over, took Philip's wrist and after a moment's feeling for the man's pulse, said, 'Too late. He's dead already.'

Cold shock! *No, Rudi was lying*!

'I can't feel his heart either,' said Rudi, and Diana knocked his hand away from Philip's chest, leaned forward and pressed her own palm flat aginst his rib cage.

After a moment she felt the faint beating vibration.

'It's feeble. But he is alive. We must do something, Rudi. We *must*.'

Rudiger Molner looked across at the distant flats. 'OK. We'll take him to a house. We'll leave him on the steps and ring the doorbell.'

Diana was incensed at the suggestion. 'Dump him? Just cast him off! After all he's done for us!'

Rudiger responded equally angrily. 'It's more important that we stay free! I'm sorry for him, but right now our choice is quite clear.'

'Not if it means he has to die, Rudi. Your choice might be clear, but mine isn't. I'm staying with him. You can drive us as near as possible to a hospital, and leave us, if that's what you want.'

'You'll be caught. Diana, I can't let you do it. What we've got is important. You know that.'

'Nothing!' she said deliberately, as cold and as assertive as possible, 'Nothing is ever so important that somebody *else* has to die. The moment Philip was hit, our priorities changed. I'm sorry, Rudi. But that's the way it is. Philip first, and the operation second. Now drive!'

And after a brief moment of glaring objection, Rudiger Molner started up the engine and turned the car back onto the road.

In the early hours of the evening, George Cowley arrived at the forensic laboratories attached to CI5. John Dodds had agreed to work late, and under high pressure, in order to analyse and evaluate the sample of cocaine that had been removed from Latimer's apartment.

Cowley was specifically interested in learning how pure the sample was, and whether or not the way it might have been 'cut' could indicate its likely source.

Dodds was not finished when Cowley arrived, and Cowley, hungry as a horse, took the opportunity to fetch a beef sandwich and a plastic cup of coffee, which he made palatable by the addition of a teaspoonful of malt whisky.

He stood, eating and drinking this inadequate and quite offensive supper, in the ante-room to the extensive laboratories. This was a place where the walls were decorated with information sheets, posters and photographs of the sort of work that went on beyond the swing doors.

What took Cowley's interest particularly this evening was the flow chart of the world's cocaine industry.

Cocaine. Officially classified as a dangerous drug, cocaine was most familiar for its use in dentistry. But on that circuit of the nouveau riche, that sub-culture of moneyed peasantry that had bought into land, and could not, now, be shaken from that wealth by anything but a socialist revolution, cocaine was the most popular stimulant available. Expensive, non-addictive, destructive to mucus membranes only if taken in excess, and by a person of inadequate intelligence who couldn't monitor his or her own vulnerability to the drug, cocaine was one of the world's most important, illegal industries. It gave rise to a chain of business that stretched from fields of coca plants, mostly in South America, via countries well set up to distribute anything from arms to drugs, from pornography to child slaves, through to the sophisticated outlets of America, Western Europe, and the Middle East.

It was a long way from the innocent jab in the dentist's chair.

Cocaine was extracted from the leaves of the coca plant, still chewed by the Indian peasantry of the South American countries that were one of the world's largest producers of both the legal and illegal versions of the leaf-extract. Legally, the extract was of use in medicine as a local anaesthetic, particularly for work on the eyes. But cocaine's most noticeable effect, to the labourers who cultivated and chewed the raw leaves, was that of a mental stimulant and hunger depressant; it had effect both on the central nervous system and on the mucus membranes of the stomach, which it could depress, thus removing the signal for 'need of food'.

The sense of alert, healthy, well-being so produced was avidly sought.

Such a sense was far from the feeling that George Cowley

was enjoying at the moment, as he swallowed the last of the dry beef, washed down with the powdered coffee. His stomach seemed to moan at him. He stared at the plastic cup in some disdain, aware for the first time of what he had actually done. Then he crumpled the cup and tossed it into a waste bin.

Swallowing as hard as possible, grimacing with the after taste of the sour, machine drink, he walked quickly through into the laboratories and made his way towards the solitary figure he could see in the distance.

John Dodds looked up as Cowley approached, nodded his head by way of acknowledgement, then continued to stare at his notepad, on which a number of pencilled words and figures were scrawled.

He was leaning forward on the workbench, arms folded across his chest. He chewed his lower lip thoughtfully, and occasionally shook his head, just enough to indicate the continuing thought processes that were occurring in his mind. In his shirtsleeves he looked quite unlike the forensic expert he was. His greying hair was unkempt, presumably from hours of running his fingers through the matted locks.

Around him, on the bench, the testing equipment was a messy confusion of beakers, tubes, Bunsen burners and colourful reagents.

'Hello George,' he said after a moment, and his unhappiness, or his confusion, whatever it was, was a palpable presence in his tone of voice.

'What's the puzzle, John? Problem not too big for you, surely?'

Dodds straightened up, still staring at his notepad. Then he shook his head, reached for a pack of cigarettes and drew one out, swivelling on his chair to face Cowley at the same time.

'Odd,' he said, and paused a moment to light his cigarette. He smiled at Cowley quickly. 'Occasionally break my own rules,' he said, exhaling smoke. 'At this time of night I need a bit of a stimulus. Nothing as strong as cocaine, of course, but we all need our little weakness.'

'I shan't report you,' said Cowley. 'So what's the

problem, John? You've been twice as long as normal on this test.'

'Twice as long as normal on a routine test for cocaine, even a routine evaluation of strength. Yes.' He smoked hard for a moment, eyes narrowed. 'But this stuff ...' he indicated the cocaine sample from Westbury Grove, and shook his head. 'This stuff is like nothing we've ever tested.'

'Meaning what?' said Cowley, slightly alarmed. 'Are you telling me ... what are you telling me? That it isn't cocaine?'

'The question – whether or not this is cocaine –' he picked up the sample, 'is slightly philosophical.'

Cowley felt a tinge of irritation with the chemist. 'In what way would that be? Speak out, man.'

Dodds said, 'Either it's cocaine, with a lot of other things added, or it's something similar to cocaine, but not *exactly* cocaine ...' he looked up at Cowley, his eyes registering his deep confusion. 'I've not come across anything like this before. Not ever. Sorry, George. You see before you one very baffled forensic chemist.'

'It couldn't just be the way it's been cut? They do cut it with other drugs, isn't that right? To make it go further?'

Dodds nodded thoughtfully. 'This stuff hasn't been cut. At least, not in the traditional ways. There is more than one component to the sample. But the whole sample doesn't respond like cut cocaine, or even pure cocaine. When I isolate the substance that responds to the cocaine separation it suddenly ...' he looked up at Cowley, eyes wide with mock puzzlement. 'It suddenly no longer behaves like cocaine.'

'Let me get this right. As far as you're concerned, assessing the sample as it stands –'

'It's cocaine,' said Dodds quickly. 'No doubt about it. Did a couple of animal tests, and it's cocaine!'

'But try and separate it, and there are components. And none of the components are cocaine itself! Is that what you're saying?'

Dodds nodded vigorously. 'That's exactly it, George. It's as if there are two – or possibly more – active substances. Neither of those active ingredients is cocaine, but combined

36

together they produce exactly the same effect!'

Cowley was astonished. 'Is that feasible?'

'If it is,' said Dodds pointedly, and quietly, 'if this sample is what I can only believe it to be, then I believe that someone has succeeded where every other chemist in the world has failed.' He looked up at Cowley.

Cowley said dully, 'Succeeded in what?' He almost knew the answer.

He was not surprised, then, when Dodds said simply, 'Someone, somewhere, has managed to make artificial cocaine.'

It wasn't hard discovering where Philip Latimer had pursued his research, even though there were no clues as to his college in the room, and Patel just knew that it was 'one of the London Colleges'.

At eight thirty in the morning, Bodie left the registrar's office, came back to the car where Doyle was waiting for him.

'Any luck?'

Bodie flopped into the seat and passed a small, beige envelope to his partner. 'Very co-operative. Everyone's on holiday, but the college has been taken over by a foreigners' language school. That's a list of their names. They let me rifle the files quite happily.'

'That's nice.' Doyle quickly scanned the list of summer students. 'Okay, we can easily crosscheck the names with the appropriate embassies.'

Bodie grinned. 'That is the general idea. You're beginning to think again, Doyle.'

Doyle scowled. 'A peaceful three month vacation, and suddenly back to you. I don't know what pains me more, my shoulder or my partner.'

'Well, you just take it easy, rest the shoulder. I'll do the hard work. And if you come up with any ideas, just pass them on.' Bodie grinned boyishly.

'It's going to be hell with you for the next few weeks. I can see it. Hell.' He folded the sheet of names back into the envelope. 'How about the dead girl's landlord?'

'All the rooms in that house are let out by the college. No landlord as such. She was a month behind with her rent, too.'

'I don't know why, but that pleases me. How about Latimer? Anything on him?'

'Same story,' said Bodie. 'Everyone on vacation. His supervising professor is on an orchid hunting expedition in Borneo.'

Doyle was impressed. 'Fancy a trip to talk to him?'

'This time of year?' Bodie's eyes glowed. 'Yeah!'

'You'll need your butterfly net.'

'It's packed and ready,' said Bodie with a smirk. 'Just think of Cowley's face: "air-fare to Borneo, please sir, it's all connected with the job."'

Mimicking Cowley's Scottish accent, Doyle said, 'May I remind you, Bodie, that CI5 is an organisation of limited funding. You'll go by raft and like it!'

Both men grinned at the image of Cowley's face when he had heard any sort of proposal that involved high budget and personnel. Then Doyle said, 'So that's it? Just the list? Nothing else on Latimer?'

'I've got his date of birth from the registrar. For what it's worth.'

Doyle took the scribbled date from Bodie, then called through to Control. 'Go ahead Four-five.'

'Can you run a check on Philip Latimer, date of birth twenty sixth August, nineteen fifty five. He's a post graduate student.' Doyle told them the name of the college and the department.

'Stand by, Four-five,' came the soft voice of the woman monitoring Control for that day.

Bodie said, with a frown as Doyle sat back to wait for the information to come through, 'Hang about. Why do I need a butterfly net for orchids?'

Looking astonished, Ray Doyle said, 'A strong boy like you – going to catch them with your fingers?'

Control called back. 'Your check is starting to come through.'

'Already?' Fast work, he was thinking. 'How much of it? A long report?'

'Quite long. Do you want me to read it out?'

Doyle exchanged a glance with Bodie, who shrugged and nodded. The early morning traffic was building up outside, the streets getting very busy.

'Go ahead.'

They listened to the facts about Philip Latimer, allowing most of the information to drain away; it was unimportant, irrelevant to the present assignment.

In fact, Latimer had led a routine life up until 1974; it was in November of that year that events started to get interesting.

'Charged in November 1974 with possession of marijuana and the growth of cannabis in his bedsit. Do you want the court summaries?'

Doyle said, 'Not for the moment. Just give us the main events.'

The woman read, 'His sentence was two years, suspended. The court listed him as a Ph.D. student, researching into Molecular Isomorphy. He was arrested during a protest outside the American embassy on July thirteenth 1978, but released without charges being pressed. In December 1979 he was photographed on an Anti-National Front march. He's also a signatory of a petition against the Escondian Military Dictatorship; the petition was prepared in February 1980. That's about it.'

Doyle looked at his partner, registering puzzlement. Escondora? Where the hell was that?

I don't know either, came Bodie's answering glance.

Doyle said, 'Okay, get that through to Alpha Control, will you? And stand by for an immigration and embassy crosscheck list. Twenty names.'

'Ready when you are.'

He drew the sheet of names from the envelope, but waited a moment before relaying them through to Control. They watched, idly, as a traffic warden worked along the row of illegally parked cars towards theirs; but they were more concerned with digesting what they had learned about Philip Latimer.

'What do you make of it?' Doyle asked. Bodie's shrug was non-committal.

'Government warning? Marijuana smoking can be dangerous to your political health.'

'You reckon every student who rolled up in the mid-seventies has been tagged and photographed ever since?'

'Doubt it.'

'So why Latimer?'

There was no immediate answer to the question. Doyle also added that, 'Latimer's background isn't the usual background for a pedlar of hard drugs.'

'A lot of money in it,' answered Bodie. 'Maybe he saw the light and decided to become a capitalist.'

'There are certainly slower ways.'

'Like working for C15.'

Doyle stared down at the list of names, then sighed. He reached for the R/T. 'Stand by, Control. Names for embassy check for authenticity. Ready?'

'Ready.'

Doyle began to read from the list. Bodie drove smoothly away from the yellow line at the side of the road, an instant before the traffic warden reached them.

Chapter Five

He had hunted throughout the night, driving quietly and slowly through the streets of London, always watching, always alert. He had moved from hospital to hospital, beginning with the smaller medical centres and casualty departments. He had reasoned that the dying youth would be taken somewhere a little less obvious than such open, busy places as the Royal Free.

He was calm as he hunted. He was almost smug. The girl had been distressed by the shooting, and the boy had been badly, but not immediately fatally shot, and at some time during the next few hours simple compassion would overrule their fear of being caught by the police, and they would seek expert help.

They would be watching for police, and would not be concentrating too hard on men in plain clothes. From a distance they would probably not recognise the man who hunted them as the man who had broken into their apartment earlier in the day.

And when he found them, Dan Harris would shoot to kill. It was his job. He didn't feel the same reluctance to administer the fatal shot as his colleague, Thomas.

So he prowled through the night, watching for his targets, calmly anticipating the moment of the kill.

His story, at each hospital, grew more refined, more clipped, the rough edges ironed out with repetition so that by the time he was checking the tenth casualty ward, he was able to state his question, and his reasons for asking the question, and get his response without arousing suspicion.

Has anyone been brought in with a gunshot wound? A boy, early twenties, with a blonde girl.

At the tenth stop the receptionist frowned slightly. She was a prim, pert woman in her forties, wearing the uniform

41

of an auxiliary nurse. 'You're the second person to ask me that in an hour,' she said. 'I've just spoken to some police department or other. Same question.'

'The kid ran away from a hospital in St Albans. He got himself into trouble earlier today, but had the sense to go to his sister's. Trouble is, his sister doesn't trust his probabtion officer as much as he did. They're in London somewhere and I need to find them. I don't want a fuss about what happened. He's on the edge already, mentally . . .'

'I see. Well, we've had nothing of that description. Not yet. Besides, all gunshot wounds are automatically reported to the local station. I'm afraid it will be impossible to fully protect your charge from publicity.'

'Thanks anyway,' said Harris, and walked from the brightly lit foyer of the hospital.

He crossed the road to his car, weary and feeling that it would soon be time to close his eyes for an hour, to snatch a refreshing cat nap.

It was an hour to dawn. He pulled the car into a side road, lay back in the driver's seat, and slept.

And at dawn he woke, his skin tingling with anticipation. He reversed the car into the main road and parked again, facing the steps at the front of the hospital. For a few minutes there was just a trickle of early morning traffic, moving towards the West End. He began to think that it had been no more than an adrenalin flush, a waking dream, a false sense of expectation.

Then the battered Renault appeared in the distance, and he smiled.

His intuition had not, after all, let him down.

As the Renault drove slowly out of the dawn, passing right by the hospital, Harris slid down in his seat, watching the vehicle through his mirror. He was ready to go in pursuit, but felt instinctively that the driver was intending to use the nearby hospital, and was just checking out the area.

Sure enough, the Renault slowed, then drove steadily around the small green opposite the hospital. It parked across the playing ground, and there it stayed for an hour or more.

Harris could see agitated activity within it. He could almost hear the argument between the girl and the boy, the need to get the wounded man into casualty versus the fear of who or what might be waiting for them inside.

Take your time, kids, he thought to himself. You've got a surprise coming, and I want you to enjoy it ...

'I think I'm beginning to hate you, Rudi.' Diana Molner spoke coldly, reaching over onto the back seat and feeling again for Philip's pulse. It was hardly there at all, the merest flicker below the skin. Philip's breathing was so shallow that repeatedly through the night Diana had thought he had died.

But each time he had rallied slightly, eyes opening, the merest hint of a smile touching his lips. And once, just once in the darkest of hours, he had whispered to Diana that he loved her.

It had made her cry. Rudi had sat and silently listened to her, but still he refused to go into a hospital. They had driven past three, and the argument had raged bitterly in the car, Diana practically wrenching the wheel of the Renault to make it run into the kerb.

Now at last Rudi was prepared to take the chance. Diana prayed that it was not too late for Philip Latimer.

He started up the engine and sidled round the park. There were a few stationary vehicles in the vicinity, but try as he might he could see no movement from any of them, and was convinced that they were deserted. The traffic began to increase in volume along the road at the front of the hospital.

There was no sign of the police.

'Now,' he said, and ran the car up onto the pavement at the bottom of the hospital steps. 'Quickly!' he said. 'Get him, leave him, out to the car and gone. We don't wait around, is that clear?'

It was suddenly happening so fast that Diana was made almost dizzy. After so many hours of argument, or just

43

sitting in the car, this sudden activity was shocking to her system. She found herself dumbly obeying her brother.

They pulled Philip's limp body from the car and carried it between them up the steps and through the swing doors.

'Help us! Somebody help us!' she called out as they came into the foyer, and a nurse and an orderly came running towards them, the orderly pushing a sheet-covered trolley.

They helped Philip to lie down and the orderly bent over him, taking the vital signs, and snapping out an instruction to fetch one of the doctors.

It was over that fast, and Rudi grabbed Diana's hand and squeezed it, whispering, 'Time to go. Just walk.'

They turned back to the swing doors, and took a single step forward. And stopped. Diana gasped with surprise, Rudi just made a growling sound, registering both his shock and his irritation.

It was one of the men who had stolen the cocaine. He was coming through the swing doors, and reaching into his inside jacket pocket. There was an arrogant, cold little smile on his lips.

'This way,' said Rudi in a desperate murmur. Hand in hand with his sister he ran back along the corridor, ignoring the nurse's voice as she called to them to stay with the man they'd brought in.

She started to give chase, but stopped as Harris roughly pushed her aside, running after the fleeing youngsters.

Rudi darted into the first door he came to, dragging his sister with him. It led into a utility corridor, and they ran swiftly along it, looking for an alternative way out of the hospital.

Behind them, the door was slammed open, and Harris's heavy footfall told of his determined pursuit.

Frantically, the two of them searched for an escape route. They ran through one of the wards, startling nurses and patients alike. They tried every door they could, but so many were locked, or just gave access to storerooms.

Diana wanted to hide in such a place, but Rudiger couldn't bear the thought of being trapped. His face dripped sweat. He no longer held her hand, and now carried the pistol, ready to shoot.

And always, behind them, was the sound of the hunter, his footfall slowing, then increasing in speed as he dogged their heels.

They came, at last, to the steps leading down to the boiler room. 'There'll be an exit to the rear yards,' said Rudi. 'Come on.'

'I don't like it!' Diana said nervously. The basement looked dark, far too quiet for her liking. But Rudi urged her, 'Come on'.

And in the distance she heard a sound like a cough, and the dark-suited figure appeared across the glass doors leading to a ward. Watching her.

Rudi led the way between the machinery, through the shadows. The basement was stuffy and stiflingly hot. The biggest of the boilers was making a bass humming sound, and the vibration in the air was unnerving and disquieting. Diana followed her brother to the large double doors that led to the exterior.

She felt a great surge of shock as she realised that they were locked. Rudi was tugging on them frantically. He had slipped the bolts at top and bottom, but there must have been a deeper locking mechanism.

'Shit!' He turned and leaned against the doors, his eyes wide with fear. He passed the pistol from hand to hand, watching the stairs that led down from ground level. There were no other exits from the basement as far as either he or Diana could see.

And the man who hunted them came stealthily, cautiously down the steps.

Diana crouched behind one of the boilers. Rudi pressed himself flat by the wall behind a concrete supporting pillar, the gun held close to his chest, his breathing as quiet as possible. He was aware that the man had reached the bottom of the steps and was peering into the gloomy utility room, seeking among the shadows for a sign of movement.

And for a minute or so there was just the silence, a silence

45

broken only by the humming of the machinery, and the occasional distant clatter of a trolley. Diana remained crouching, her head bowed, ready to run at the first shot. Rudi stared ahead of him, letting the sweat pour from his scalp and down his face. Some instinct in him told him that the other man was very, very close by.

It happened then, and it happened so fast that Diana could only scream and try to piece together retrospectively what had occurred.

Crouched and quiet she had looked up, and on looking up had seen the dark-suited man standing behind the pillar where Rudi was hiding.

The man saw her and flung himself away from the pillar towards the floor, twisting as he jumped and shooting towards the place where Rudi was standing.

If Rudi had only kept still the shot would have bounced off concrete, but Rudi Molner was spooked by the sudden alarm he'd seen in his sister's face.

He stepped out of cover, twisting to fire.

His finger had hardly tightened on the trigger of his pistol before Harris's shot took him high on the body, ripping into his right chest and blasting him backwards. He struck the wall and his face grimaced with pain, but no sound came from his lips.

Diana just screamed. Two men in twenty four hours, two men that she loved ... She lost all sense of self-protection, clasped her hands to her mouth and stood.

Grinning as he climbed to his feet, Harris turned towards her and easily, almost disinterestedly raised his gun, sighting along it, ready to dispatch her with a single shot through the head.

Rudi slumped slowly to the ground, a thin trickle of blood emerging from his mouth. As he slumped he suddenly found a moment's strength, raised his own gun again and shot Harris neatly through the heart.

Harris span in shock, eyes narrowing, hand touching his breast. His mouth gaped, his head shook as if to say, 'It's not possible. I just blew you away, kid. You're not strong enough to shoot from that close to death.'

Then he toppled forward, the magnum clattering onto the concrete floor. His hand scrabbled for the gun, but Diana Molner stepped quickly over and picked it up. When she ran to her brother she was aware that the dying man had produced a small walkie-talkie from his jacket pocket and was trying to operate it with one hand.

He died before he could say a word, his face freezing with its eyes open, his finger still touching the small green contact button.

Rudi was gasping for breath, the pain he was feeling very evident in the way his face contorted each time he tried to move.

'Oh God, Rudi. Not you too . . .'

'Shut up,' he said sharply, gasping for breath as he snapped out the words. 'Help me up.'

'What have we got ourselves into,' she moaned quietly as she struggled to help her brother to his feet. Blood poured from the bullet wound. In seconds she was coated with it.

'Give me the magnum,' he said grimly, and he weighed it heavily in his hand, leaning on her as he limped towards the locked rear doors.

He raised the gun and blew a hole through the strange lock. The doors blew open and Diana Molner helped him out into the bright day.

They staggered across the yard, between the huge dustbins of refuse, and the piled crates of empty bottles of varying sorts, and made their way towards the open gates, out of the hospital grounds.

As they came to the pavement, Rudi shook Diana off and lurched unsteadily out into the road, one hand clutching at his shoulder, the other waving the heavy duty pistol. A car screeched to a stop and Rudiger Molner pushed the barrel of the pistol through the driver's window and shouted, 'If you don't want to get hurt, just do what I tell you.'

The driver looked terrified. He stared helplessly at the bleeding man who was challenging him, then stared at Diana as she ran into the road and quickly climbed into the passenger seat. Rudi got in behind, holding the gun menacingly against the man's spine.

'Just drive until I tell you to stop.'

'Wh ... where? Where shall I drive?' stuttered the terrified man. Rudi just jabbed him with the gun.

'Don't say another word. Just drive. I don't want to hear you speak. Clear?'

The man nodded dumbly. Diana wanted to reassure him, but she felt that Rudi might turn hostility on her as well if she did, and in his present state of mind, and with the effect on his body of the gaping wound, Rudi might have been capable of anything.

As the car lurched off down the road, Diana stared back out of the rear window.

The hijack had not gone unnoticed.

When the call to the hospital came, Bodie and Doyle were only a mile away, cruising west. Bodie was behind the wheel and he span that wheel, grunting with satisfaction as the Capri performed an immaculate U-turn, slotted neatly into the opposing traffic, and left the irate taxi, that had been forced to slow, a distant memory in just a few seconds.

They pulled up before the hospital to find a substantial police presence already in occupation. The battered Renault, parked right on the pavement near to the hospital steps, was ringed off with tape, and two uniformed men stood guard. Doyle called through the registration to Control. As he spoke into the R/T he peered through the car's windows and saw the great smear of blood on the back seat.

Then he followed Bodie into the casualty foyer, where he found a small group of police gathered around the dead body of a young man, laid out below a sheet on one of the hospital trolleys.

'What have we got?' asked Doyle, and Bodie held up a wallet, a comb and some newspaper cuttings.

In the wallet there was a driving licence in the name of Philip Latimer. Bodie called this information through to Control, while Doyle asked one of the orderlies, 'How'd he die?'

'Chest wound, too close to the heart. Loss of blood. The

couple who brought him in had left it too late. He was shot a good few hours ago, I'd say. He was dead at midnight, only he didn't quite know it.'

Doyle asked, 'Where's the other one?'

'This way.'

The orderly led them down the corridor, to the boiler room in the basement. As Doyle stepped into the humid atmosphere he could smell the acrid after-effect of a shooting, the pungent odour that always lingered.

A chalk mark had been scrawled around the body of the man. He lay, his arm outstretched, his eyes open. Blood had drained from his mouth and pooled around his head.

'Nasty,' said Bodie. 'Right through the heart, if my anatomy is up to scratch.'

'Accurate shooting, anyway,' agreed Doyle. The dead man was no kid, nor was he blond. One of the kids had done this to him, and had taken a wounding in the process.

Doyle examined the blood smear on the nearby wall. It reminded him of the pattern back at the apartment, where the girl had been blown away and slipped to the floor.

A hit from a magnum could do that to a body. But this body had got up and walked away after being shot.

They had spent a day carrying around the body of Philip Latimer. Now, one of them was hit and the whole process would begin again.

But this time there weren't two of them helping, only one. They would be like wounded animals at bay.

Potential killers.

Bodie said, 'No ID on him. Nothing at all. Clean as a whistle, and that makes me very suspicious. And what about this?'

He had picked up the small walkie-talkie, using a tissue, having eased it from between the dead man's fingers. Doyle used a pencil to pick up the thirty-eight calibre pistol that lay close to the blood smear on the wall.

He sniffed the barrel. 'Murder weapon,' he said dully, as he walked to Bodie and peered at the communications set. 'Well, well.'

Bodie said, 'Sort of looks familiar doesn't it.'

'Obsolete model tricked up with new gimmickry in an attempt to save money.' Doyle shook his head, smiling cynically. 'It's a dead giveaway every time.'

Bodie used his own R/T to call George Cowley, moving up into the ground level corridor before he could establish contact.

'Latimer dead?' Cowley repeated. 'That's a shame. Someone is playing a very deadly game, and I don't think it's the kids.'

'Definitely not,' said Bodie, watching as a nurse wheeled the trolley containing Latimer's body towards the mortuary. Someone had clearly decided to use the hospital's facilities to make their examination of the corpse. 'We've got another body on the floorboards,' Bodie went on. 'But there could be a dead rat underneath.'

Cowley's voice was cautiously interested, as if he had half suspected what would come next, but hoped to be wrong. 'What does that mean ... exactly?'

'The body is probably that of the man who shot Latimer. There's no ID on him, and I suspect the kids took his gun when they escaped ... one of *them* wounded, too. No ID, no gun, but he seems to have been carrying a Secret Service walkie-talkie.'

'Good God,' was all Cowley said, restrained, but clearly affected deeply. 'I might have known!'

As Cowley broke the contact with Bodie, the young woman sitting behind the information console called to him. 'I'm getting facts about the Renault 16.'

Cowley walked over and peered over her shoulder at the grey green with the words flickering into view as the computer discovered them. The woman read, 'There you go. Renault 16, licence number XTS 456N, registered in the name of Diana Molner. Licence number ... and there's her date of birth, third May, nineteen sixty.'

Cowley nodded as he digested the simple information, then straightened up. 'Give me a security check on the girl right away. Diana Molner,' he said, repeating the name.

It rang no bells. He was convinced that CI5 and Miss Molner had not crossed paths before.

But then, if she'd only been born in nineteen sixty there hadn't exactly been much time for such an interlinking of lives.

So young, he thought grimly. So young to be so involved with such a trade as cocaine ... so young to be pursued by the Secret Service!

He was disturbed by the news from Bodie. Just because the dead man had been carrying a piece of Secret Service issue machinery, of course, didn't mean that he *was* in the employ of the British Government. Purloined, smuggled, traded, copied; there were many ways in which a man could disguise his criminal identity, making himself seem more official than was in fact the case.

But something about this whole operation had been making Cowley edgy; things had not felt right. The rat, to which Bodie had so eloquently referred, had begun to register on Cowley's sensitive nostrils some hours before.

The damned Secret Service! What the hell was their business in the world of cocaine?

A few moments later the woman at the information bank called him back over. She was frowning slightly, puzzled by what was flashing up onto her screen.

'I'm getting an unusual code reading on Diana Molner,' she said, leaning forward slightly, then keying in an instruction again. The same information came up and she leaned back in her chair, glanced up at George Cowley.

'It's a classified read-out,' she said. 'What threw me was that it must have *just* been classified. Not all the information had been taken over.'

'What classification?' Cowley asked solemnly.

'A9,' she replied. 'We have no access at all.'

'A9,' Cowley repeated slowly, his eyes narrowed to slits, making him look both thoughtful and angry. He glanced down at the screen again, 'Is that the only Molner?'

'No,' she said. 'There's another. Male. Born Nineteen sixty one. Rudiger Molner, Diana Molner's brother.'

'What do you read on him?'

The woman shrugged. 'Just: "refer to Molner, Diana".
That and his date of birth. Someone has tied the computer
up very nicely on the two of them.'

Deeply intrigued, Cowley walked back to the phone. He
patched a call through to Doyle. 'This is Alpha One.'

'Go ahead Alpha ...'

'I'm giving you all available units, Four-five. You've got
to find those kids, and you've got to find them fast. I said fast
and I _mean_ fast. And whatever happens, I want them alive.
Is that understood? I want them both alive!'

'Got it, Alpha One. Will pass on to the driver. Out.'

Chapter Six

Too much, too fast!

Diana Molner clung to the seat of the car, her attention so divided between the ashen-faced driver, and the tears of fear that were coursing down his face, and the demonic man who sat behind, his lips drawn back and in a death-like smile, his eyes red, wide, manic, that she began to feel dizzy.

She wanted to sleep. God, how she wanted sleep. And she wanted to cry, to shed tears for Philip. She needed to cry so badly that for a moment her lips quivered, and her eyes misted over, but she held back, keeping strong.

Philip!

He was dead. He had to be dead. Rudi had seen to that, refusing to get him to a hospital for so many hours, slapping her violently in the face when she had tried to exert authority over him. He was strong; he was going mad. Even before he had been shot, his mind had been going. The shock of what had happened in Westbury Grove, the shock of seeing someone so violently killed, of realising that he had been the cause . . . all of that had made his tail go up, and he was behaving just like a violent, hunted animal.

Now he was wounded, and dangerous to everyone.

And Philip was dead. Calm Philip, reassuring Philip. Philip, who could have handled Rudi so well, taken the weapon from him, worked out the consequences of any action, and taken them – so calmly! – to where they would need to go. Philip was dead. Even though he had been breathing as they had helped him into the hospital, one last, loving glance at him as they had lain him on the trolley had been enough to confirm her worst fears.

Philip had smiled at her, just briefly, and then all the tension had gone from his face and his eyes had closed.

Too busy, at the time, to recognise death for what it was,

now that slight smile haunted her. To have kissed his lips, just once, just one last time ...

And she had been running for her life, while Philip had slipped away.

Rudi's breathing was loud, difficult. He sounded like an animal, like a beast of prey, panting after the hunt. He snapped out instructions to the terrified driver, accompanying the words with violent jabs of the gun to the man's neck. 'Right down here! Do it! Next left!'

The driver was shaking, muffing his gear-changes, repeatedly wiping his palms against his jacket. For him, the initial dryness of shock and terror had passed into a sweaty anticipation of the final bullet that would leave him slumped across the wheel as his unwelcome passengers made good their getaway.

It was too much for Diana. As the car lurched and swerved, and her body bounced against the door and the dash-board, she said, 'You'll be all right. We won't hurt you.'

'Shut up!' screamed Rudi, and pointed the gun at her.

'Shut up yourself Rudi,' she said back, cool and hostile. 'The man's terrified of what you'll do to him. But I'm not going to let you kill him.'

'Thank you,' whispered the driver, then grimaced as the cold mouth of the pistol touched his neck again.

'Just drive and keep quiet!' Rudiger snapped, but Diana's sudden confrontation had taken the edge from his anger.

And abruptly he cried out, 'Right, stop the car!'

The man needed no second bidding. They were in a long, straight road, and there was no-one in immediate sight, although distantly there were shops and a trickle of shoppers.

Diana jumped from the car, came round and helped Rudi to stagger out. His chest was saturated with blood, but he was not anywhere near as badly wounded as Philip had been. He kept the gun pointed at the sweating driver all the time. 'Drive on! *Fast*! Don't turn off this road for a mile, is that clear?'

54

'Yes!' said the driver loudly, and turned to cast a quick, searching glance at Rudiger Molner.

The man was in his forties, soft-faced, soft-eyed, full-lipped and rather ordinary. But that momentary look was charged with hate. It was the traditional look that could have killed, and it shocked Diana, and made Rudi stiffen slightly in her grasp.

Then the car had screeched away, exhaust fumes dense and white, tyres burning on the tarmac roadway.

Rudi grabbed Diana by the hand and raced with her through an alleyway. For a man with a bullet hole through him he was suddenly very strong. But Diana knew that it was probably his last burst of energy before a more fatal weakness set in.

'Rudi, this is mad! Where are you going?'

'Just run. Keep quiet and run. Give me your coat to hide the blood.'

'Where are we going?'

'A hotel! Come on!'

And with a last quick look back at the road, Diana followed her brother's lurching body, catching him up again and reaching out a steadying hand as they moved.

Back at Control, George Cowley paced restlessly, thinking hard, waiting for something – anything – that might give him an idea of why the Secret Service were involved with the Molner couple. And waiting, too, for news of the brother and sister team themselves.

Bodie and Ray Doyle, in Bodie's Capri, were now searching the area around the hospital, moving towards the logical place where Rudiger Molner might have headed, the borough where Philip Latimer had had his apartment, the quiet, run down streets of that part of London where it was possible to lose yourself quite easily.

The controller called to Cowley and he walked across to her. 'Well?'

'I've just checked the coding on the Molner girl. A9.

Unusual classification. And it turns out to belong to the Foreign Office.'

'What department?' asked Cowley, but the girl just shrugged.

'We don't have that logged, I'm afraid.' She looked up at Cowley. 'Could the Foreign Office have planted the D-One with us?'

'It's a distinct possibility. If only we knew what game they were playing.'

The Foreign Office, he thought bitterly. CI5 had always had a good relationship with the F.O., but neither department was ever totally honest with the others. And the F.O.'s dirty tricks department was rumoured to be among the dirtiest around.

A9. An F.O. classification that Cowley had not come across. And an F.O. department that would shoot students on home ground in cold blood.

It stank. As far as Cowley was concerned it smelled so bad that something would have to be done, and soon.

From a different console in the Operations room, a man called to Cowley, 'We've got a report of a car hijacking coming in.' For a second Cowley hesitated, not sure whether or not this was of relevance to the Molner case.

Then the monitor announced, 'From outside the Northgate Hospital.'

'That's them!' said Cowley quickly. 'What's the registration?'

But that information was not available. The woman who had phoned the report through had waited a long time, not sure of what it was she had seen. She had been working in the hospital kitchens, had even heard the sound of a gunshot, but had hesitated to 'get involved'.

Cowley was briefly frustrated, then asked, 'The make of the car?'

'Brown,' came the reply from the monitor. On the screen that single, useless piece of information stood there, a challenge to sanity.

'Damn!' said Cowley.

And then:

'Hold it ... another report coming through.'

The words flickered up onto the screen. And this time Cowley smiled, exhaling loudly with satisfaction.

He snatched up the phone, calling through to both Bodie and Doyle.

'We've got them,' he said. 'They hijacked a car outside the hospital. The driver let them off five minutes ago in Beauford Road.'

Across the R/T Cowley could hear the sound of wheels screeching, as one or other of the CI5 men put his car into a U-turn, to race to the scene.

Cowley added, 'Rudiger and Diana Molner. The man is armed, wounded, and very dangerous. The driver said he thinks he's going slowly mad. The sister is helping him, but seems to be distraught. Probably the death of the Latimer boy. So play on Diana's reason. They're on foot now, and can't get far.'

'And keep them alive,' came Doyle's voice, and Cowley nodded grimly.

'At all costs, Four-five. At all costs.'

Joe Thomas stepped from the concealment of a shop doorway, crossed the road carefully, weaving his way between the traffic, and walked along the small side-street in Ealing. He glanced behind him as he walked, then drew out a pair of dark glasses and put them on.

The man who was walking ahead of him slowed his pace, and they met up and walked side by side, not looking at each other.

Northcott said, 'Why did you want to see me?'

Thomas shook his head. 'It's starting to look bad. I think it might be time to review our approach.' He glanced at Northcott. 'I'm not happy about the killing.'

Saying nothing for a second, Northcott slowed his pace even more. 'How bad do you mean?'

'For a start, CI5 is closing in on them. I don't like to tangle with that bunch.'

Northcott sneered. 'How close is closing in? Have they located the Molner girl yet?'

'Not yet,' said Thomas wearily. 'But it's only a matter of time.'

'And what about Harris? Last I heard from you he was about to intercept. What went wrong?'

'He got killed,' said Thomas. 'The boy shot him. That's what I assume, anyhow. He didn't check in after going in for the kill, and I heard gunfire over his transmitter. He left it switched on so I could hear the encounter.'

'Harris dead,' Northcott repeated, 'And Thomas becoming windy ...'

'It's not a question of that,' said Thomas irritably. 'I told you up front that I didn't like the idea of killing them.'

'That's a shame,' said Northcott. 'At least Harris won't talk.'

Thomas said, 'His fingerprints will. Straight to the Department.'

'I can take care of that. How about CI5? You have a tail on them?'

'Yes,' said Thomas. 'They're too busy hunting for the kids to look behind them. I've got two men on the job.'

'Something done right,' said Northcott sarcastically. 'Okay, stick close to CI5. Let them lead you to the Molner kids, and pick them off whenever you get the chance.'

He stopped walking, stared hard at Joe Thomas. The dislike and uncertainty in Thomas's eyes was powerfully visible, and Northcott was uneasy at putting so much trust in this man. 'You *will* pick them off ... or get one of the others to do it?'

'I'll do it,' said Thomas.

'I'm glad to hear it.'

Northcott didn't add that if Thomas failed to extinguish the two troublesome lives, he still had another big card to play.

The hotel was small and dingy, the rooms smelling slightly of damp. The windows were stiff to move, and the room that Rudiger Molner had taken looked out over junk-ridden backyards. It was a place he had used on and off over the last few months. His face was familiar to the manager, and he had been able to enter without suspicion, even though he was patently very ill.

Now Rudi waited just inside the door, the pistol in his hand; he was pressed against the door jam, listening to the murmur of voices outside.

When Diana came back into the room, she was leading a middle-aged man, short of stature, rather gruff in his general demeanour. Rudi was behind the door, and he slammed it shut, causing the older man to react with surprise.

'Doctor ... Roberts?'

'Yes,' said the man, then looked pointedly at the pistol that Rudiger was holding. 'Is that really necessary?'

'I'll decide things like that. All you need worry about is helping me. Have you brought everything you need?'

Doctor Roberts bristled slightly at the arrogance in the young man. 'I believe I have,' he said. 'Perhaps you'd better lie down.'

Rudi limped towards the bed, collapsed heavily onto it in a sitting position, then slowly lay down. He kept the pistol trained on the doctor all the time. Roberts angrily pushed the pistol aside as he leaned towards the wounded man, but Rudi jerked it back and breathed, 'Don't touch the gun! Just see to my wound!'

Diana stood by the window, her arms crossed, her face looking anxious and wan. 'Is he going to be all right?' she asked, and Doctor Roberts sighed with irritation.

'Please!' he said. 'Let me examine the man first.'

He loosened and removed the bandages from around Rudi's chest, took a long hard look at the wounding, then shook his head. He replaced the bandages and tightened them again. Rudi watched him, frowning. 'What are you doing?'

'I'm replacing the bandages.'

'I can see that. I mean why? How can you clean the wound through the rags?'

'I'm not even going to attempt to,' said Roberts quietly. He had straightened up, very conscious of the pistol that was waveringly pointed at his stomach.

'I told you to help me!'

'You've got to get to hospital, Mr Molner. I really am not equipped to deal with wounding like that.'

'I said fix it! You!' Rudi pushed the gun against the doctor's belly, and swung his legs from the bed. Diana stepped away from the window. 'Rudi! Stop being so hostile. And put the gun down, for Christ's sake. He's only trying to do what's best for you.'

Rudiger Molner glared at the implacable doctor. His face began to twist with rage again, the skin breaking out into a fine sweat. 'I said, Doctor, that I want you to help me.'

'I can't,' insisted Roberts.

'Do something or I shoot!'

'No, Rudi!' shouted Diana, then she turned to Doctor Roberts and implored. 'Please! Do what you can! Just clean and change the bandages.'

Roberts glanced at her, then down at the pistol. Then he nodded, reached for his black bag again and drew out several pieces of medical equipment, including a syringe and a small vial of morphine.

'No injections,' said Rudiger flatly. Roberts hesitated as he was filling the syringe.

'It's just something for the pain.'

'Forget the pain.'

'And you need glucose . . .'

'Forget it. No injections.'

Doctor Roberts shrugged. 'Very well.' He placed the syringe back in the bag, brought out some elastic bandages, then unwound the bandages from Rudi's body. Rudi lay back, allowing the wound to be probed, cleaned.

Suddenly Roberts straightened up again, deeply perturbed. 'Good God man! This is far more serious than it looks.'

'*DO WHAT YOU CAN!*' screeched Rudi.

'I can't stop bleeding when its internal! You've ruptured a main vessel, man! You're bleeding to death. You *must* have hospital treatment!'

Diana flung her hands to her mouth to stifle the sound of shock. She had screwed up her eyes, and was fighting not to cry. 'Rudi . . .' she finally managed to say. 'Please God, have some sense. I can't lose you too!'

'Come on, man,' said Roberts firmly. 'You must get to hospital immediately. They can help you more than I can.'

But Rudiger Molner shook his head. 'How much time do I have?'

'I really don't know. I'd have to take your blood pressure.'

'Then take it! Quick! I want to know how long I've got!' He glanced at Diana, then at the door. 'Keep a watch out, Diana. Keep watching.'

Roberts picked up the black bladder and wrapped it round Rudi's arm, pumping it up and watching the pressure figures. After a moment he shrugged, let the bladder deflate then rolled it up and placed it back in the bag.

Rudiger knew the answer, and sighed almost with relief, settling back on the bed. 'Not very long, I take it.'

Roberts just said, 'I don't even know if a hospital could save you now. You've lost too much. You must be mad, you must have lost your mind, that's all I can say.'

Rudiger Molner struggled up to a sitting position. 'Yes, well that's as may be. Now you can help me to a taxi, and your task is done.'

'Where are we going now?' asked Diana hopefully. 'You're going to let us take you to a hospital?'

'No way. Help me!'

Between them, they helped Rudi down the stairs to the street, where Diana hailed a taxi then helped her brother to climb in. Doctor Roberts stood watching them go, then shook his head and went back into the hotel to call the police. He had seen dead men before, but it was chilling to see one still so lively.

'Land of a thousand bedsitters . . .' said Ray Doyle, as Bodie skidded the Capri into the kerb, almost at the spot where the hijacked car had been let go. The man had described the area of London well. Doyle noticed that there were many alleyways and side-streets leading off from both sides of the road.

'Bedsitters,' asked Bodie, 'And hotels. That's where

they'll have been going. Some tiny hotel, top floor, smell of rubbish, indifferent management. Pay your money, do what you like.'

Doyle nodded his agreement, staring around at the area. 'It'd take too long to check everywhere. He had enough strength left to run a fair way, according to the bloke he got to drive him here.'

'And Diana helping him.'

Ray Doyle picked up the R/T and called Control. 'Entering the haystack,' he said. 'Eyes skinned for needles.'

Bodie slid the car into gear and kerb crawled, then turned first left, studying every street, every window in every house. There were several cars about, but Bodie suddenly made a sound like a man who has just realised something. His gaze was fixed on the driving mirror and Doyle glanced backwards. 'What is it?'

'Grey saloon. Two cars back. Ugly looking car . . . thought so the first time I saw it.'

Doyle spotted the vehicle in question. 'Yeah,' he said. 'I think we've passed it earlier.'

'Near the hospital,' Bodie added, the image of seeing the car coming back to him quite strongly.

'By the roundabout.'

Ray Doyle straightened in his seat, boyish features set firm, almost pouting as he thought of what the tail could mean. 'Secret Service?'

Bodie shrugged, dark eyes twinkling. 'Can out-run an old crate like that. Just wonder who it is.'

Before Doyle could comment further, the R/T sounded. The controller's voice was crisp as she said, 'Four-five, Three-seven, we have another sighting in your area. Outside the Brent Hotel, Albion Street. Subjects confirm very positively to description of the Molners. Go to it.'

Doyle scanned the pages of the street finder, oriented himself quickly then said, 'Left at these lights.'

The car rocketed forward as Bodie's right foot rammed to the floor. Behind them the grey saloon speeded up too. The controller said, 'Suspects were set down by a cab at 12.21 hours. That's seven minutes ago.'

'Right,' said Doyle, and added to Bodie, 'Still a bloody big haystack.'

The computer control room at CI5 had been a hive of activity for most of the morning. Cowley had prowled the length of it, checking and re-checking, calling friends at the Foreign Office, and the Home Office, trying to identify the strange coding within the restrictive code A9. The 'negative access' key had read 577B, but no-one, in any department, recognised that key – or was admitting to it.

Shortly after twelve midday, the computer operator, who had been scanning name index files for anything relating to the Molners, came up with a 'Molner reference'.

George Cowley stared across the man's shoulder at the screen as he punched up information. 'It *may* be something,' the man said quietly, then sat back to let Cowley read more easily, but spoke aloud the facts that appeared there. 'Alexander Molner. Graduated· from Sandhurst in 1950, on a requisition from the Escondian Government.'

'What category is that under?' Cowley said, referring to the file source of the information. The controller smiled thinly. 'Left wing sympathies, believe it or not. Home Office file, probably too old to have been checked when the information block went up on Molners in general.'

Cowley nodded thoughtfully. 'Have you checked S.I.S. about the Escondian Military?'

'Yes I have. But there's no record.'

'Right.' Cowley straightened, tapped the man on the shoulder. 'Find out our level of diplomatic contact with the Escondian regime. South American Military junta, I believe, so we may have very tenuous links with them.'

'Yes sir.'

'And see if you can trace where Alexander Molner is now. If he's still alive, and still in uniform, he could be in quite a senior position.'

The controller asked, 'Shall I try Army Intelligence?'

'Yes. A left winger at Sandhurst, not exactly a stereotype.'

And then, a few minutes later, the identity of the restriction coding came through.

The two computer controllers were working harder than they had ever worked, and the woman who was monitoring reports from the police about the possible movement of the Molners had been giving Bodie and Doyle repeated updates on sightings, by taxi-cabs in particular. The Molners' plan was clear. They were darting across North London, trying to throw off any possible pursuit.

They would be making for a tiny, out-of-the-way hotel, there to hole-up for a while.

Eyewitnesses had confirmed that the male suspect was wounded, armed and dangerous. Doctor Roberts had called in, and had admitted that Rudiger Molner's injuries would be fatal if not immediately treated.

Now the key was broken. A9 restriction 577B had been traced to Foreign Office Department M17.

'Is that confirmed?' asked Cowley grimly. 'You're sure it's M17?'

'I double checked it myself,' said the controller. 'It's the one, all right.'

'Who's the department chief?'

'A man called Northcott. Raoul Northcott.'

'I see.' Cowley turned away, hands clasped behind his back. 'Department M17. DDT. I suppose I should have known. I suppose it was obvious all along?'

'What's DDT?' asked the controller, puzzled.

Cowley glanced round at him and smiled, though he felt less like smiling than getting on the phone to try and find out what the hell M17 was up to, interfering with a D-One drugs operation. 'DDT? It's a light-hearted epithet for what M17 is all about. The Department of Dirty Tricks.'

The controller grinned, then grew solemn. The name may have been a joke, but the work of the Department included very little that was a laughing matter.

Cowley said, 'I want you to trace a man called Somerfield. He works in Security Liaison. His name won't be listed in any of their Sections, but he's there, somewhere, and I must see him. If you come up against solid resistence, let me know immediately.'

'Right.'

George Cowley picked up the phone. 'Patch me through to Four-five.'

After a moment Doyle's voice answered.

'This is Alpha One. You may not be aware of it, but you're not alone.'

'We're aware of it,' Doyle said. 'We're keeping a low profile.'

'Good. You should anticipate interference from your friend. Interference with maximum prejudice.'

'Roger, Alpha. Four-five out.'

Chapter Seven

Moving through the area where Diana and Rudi Molner had last been seen, Ray Doyle used a loud-speaker, attached to the roof of Bodie's car, to try and get a message through to the girl. Curious shoppers watched the red Capri as it crawled past, up one street, down the next, the two youthful men inside looking hard and tired.

It was a very long shot, but those were the only shots left to play, short of the Molners making a new taxi contact: all cabs had now been alerted to the couple, but as the alert had gone out, so the Molners had chosen that moment to dive for final cover.

They were somewhere in the area, probably holed up in one of the endless house-sized hotels that littered this particular part of North London.

Doyle's message was simple, and he was growing tired of repeating it:

'Attention Diana Molner! This is CI5. We know you are in the area and your life is in danger. Telephone the following number and you will be afforded the full protection of the British Government! This is the number: three seven three zero zero two nine. I repeat, your life is in danger and you *must* trust CI5. Telephone that number, Diana. Telephone it *now!*'

A pause while the car drove slowly on, licking his lips, taking a breath, then starting again:

'Attention Diana Molner. We know you are in the area . . .' At first she thought it was one or other of the political parties, parading the streets, trying to encourage support. The drone of the loudspeaker was fascinating, and she went to the window of the small room and peered out into the crowded street.

It was a red car, with a small loud-hailer attached to its

roof. Behind her, as she watched its approach, Rudi groaned, then murmured incoherent words as his head turned from side to side. He was on the bed, covered in a blanket. The gun was still clasped firmly in his right hand. He looked deathly white, and was becoming delirious.

Diana glanced at the phone beside him. He had grasped it when he had sat on the bed, and hugged it to his chest, determined that she should not call for help.

Diana could no longer understand the reason for his reluctance to be helped, to give himself up. Perhaps she had never truly known her brother.

The operation had begun well. She was commited and prepared to die for the case in which she and Rudi had become entangled with Philip Latimer. She expected to die. Certainly. But she could no longer see the point of letting Rudi just drift into oblivion. What good was served by his insistence that the police should never take them?

The operation was effectively dead. There would be others later, with other plans. There was nothing left to be lost; nothing more that could be gained.

And she herself had lost something for which she had cared a great deal. She had lost Philip. Her political strength had never wavered through meeting Philip Latimer; rather, he had added to that strength, he had enriched her political life. He had given her the human love that can empower anything, no matter how difficult, how amoral, how ultimately deadly.

She felt so much sadness, and so much confusion. There would be time, later, for a very real grief. Now there was just the waiting: the waiting for Rudi to become so weak that he would relinquish the gun, and the phone, and let her lead him to the medical care he so desperately needed.

And, like Philip, it would probably be too late.

The car passed below the hotel window, the words booming loud from the speaker.

And she heard her name!

With a quick, guilty glance at Rudi, who had heard the name too and was suddenly quite still, eyes open and staring at the ceiling, she raised the window and leaned out.

'Attention Diana Molner,' the man at the microphone was saying. 'We know you are in the area. Your lives are in danger. Your companion is in urgent need of hospital treatment, otherwise he will soon be dead! You will be given the full protection of Her Majesty's Government. Ring this number: three seven three zero zero two nine . . .'

Startled, confused, she nevertheless memorised the number quickly. The car slipped away down the street. A second car, a grey saloon, followed it at a distance, and when that car too had gone from sight she pulled back in from the window and closed it.

She looked at Rudi, who was watching her weakly, his eyes almost closed.

Three seven three zero zero two nine.

"*NO!*"

'Rudi, let me phone them!'

'*NO!*'

'They'll help you, Rudi. You heard them. They'll afford us protection. Let me phone them . . .'

The hand that held the gun flopped from his chest to his side. Diana tensed up, wondering if he would have the resolve, or even the strength, to shoot her. But the hand remained still. Weakly, he said, 'Diana . . . don't you understand . . . they mustn't find out *anything*! Not even a hint of what we were doing. There will be others . . . others to complete the task we failed to achieve . . . Diana, I *want* to die. Then it will be up to you. Start again . . .'

He continued to talk, but the words faded into incoherency. His eyes closed and slowly his lips ceased to move, the sound of words fading into a laboured, deathly breathing. Diana watched him, then took a step towards him.

Rudiger Molner jerked his hand up, his head straining to lift from the pillow. For a moment the gun pointed at her, and his eyes shone with a sudden violent hate for her. She froze, her heart thundering.

'Rudi . . .' she whispered, her gaze mostly on the white, tense finger that curled around the gun's trigger.

'Betray . . .' he said, and choked on the word, and on saliva

68

that trickled back into his throat. His eyes closed again and he fell back onto the pillow. The pistol hand seemed to relax, the fingers loosening on the trigger and the butt.

Diana walked over to him, quite calm now. His breathing was unsteady. She felt his pulse. It was barely registering. Carefully, but firmly, she extricated the pistol from his cold fingers and placed it out of reach on a table. Then she tugged the phone from his other hand, unwound the lead from around his arm, and sat back on her haunches by the bed. She was suddenly tearful. She wiped her eyes, then cried quite loudly for a second, hugging the phone to her breast, screwing up her eyes.

Betrayer. He had been trying to call her a betrayer. But I'm not, Rudi. I'm not betraying you. I have to do this. I love you too much not to.

She picked up the receiver and listened to the dialling tone. Then, her hand shaking badly, she dialled the number that she had memorised.

After a moment the phone was answered. It was a man's voice, deep, quite gruff, with a pronounced Scottish accent. He said, 'This is George Cowley, CI5.'

She said nothing for a moment. In the background she could hear whirring and clicking sounds, also voices, which stopped at a whispered command from someone at the other end of the line.

At last she found the courage to speak. 'This is Diana Molner. I've just heard your broadcast.'

She knew she sounded weary. She found she could not put any inflection or feeling into her voice. She was dull, her tone flat, almost soporific. The tension and anxiety of the last few hours had taken its toll.

'Miss Molner,' said George Cowley gently. 'I'm very glad to have heard from you. This agency is a Security Agency. CI5. We have your welfare at heart. If you tell us where you are I shall have my men come and pick you up.'

'You said you would give us protection,' she said. 'Protection from who? From the men who killed Philip?'

'From anybody who wishes you harm, Miss Molner,' said Cowley. 'I have two men listening in to this call now. They

69

are on the street, not far from you. Just tell me where you are and they will come.'

Rudi shifted restlessly in unconsciousness, moaning slightly. Diana felt terribly uneasy, very afraid. 'How can I believe you?' she said, but really didn't mean to ask that question at all. She had no choice. She would trust anybody. She had to end this nightmare.

Cowley said, 'You have to trust me, Miss Molner. And you must believe me when I say that your lives are in danger, and that we shall protect you to the best of our ability.'

'Rudi . . . my brother . . .' she stared at the poor boy's ashen features. 'He's terribly hurt.'

Cowley was reassuring, yet firm. 'We've spoken to the doctor – Doctor Roberts – who treated your brother. He must be taken to hospital now or he will die.'

She looked down at the phone. The word 'death' rattled around her mind, seemed to scream at her from the darkness of her confusion.

'Will you promise me that he'll be taken to hospital?'

'I give you my word,' said Cowley. 'Now tell where you are.'

'He needs blood,' said Diana. 'He's lost so much blood, he needs plasma . . . something, anything . . .'

'We have an ambulance already approaching your area, Miss Molner. We have everything ready. We have a surgical team standing by. Tell me where you are. Is it a hotel? Miss Molner, are you still there? Can you hear me?'

Diana had slumped forward, racking with silent sobs. Try as she might she couldn't speak and she covered the mouthpiece of the phone for a few seconds until her wave of misery had passed. Cowley was still there, still insistantly asking for her.

'What else can I do?' she said to Rudi, still covering the mouthpiece. 'I *must* do it, Rudi. What else can I do? I'm not betraying you ... I'm *not* betraying you ...'

'Miss Molner,' Cowley was saying. 'Trust me. Please trust me. Hello? Hello?'

'Yes,' she said quietly into the phone. 'Yes, I'm still here. We're at the Flora Hotel, on Bonnington Street. We're in

70

Room 25. There's just the two of us.'

There was a brief pause and Diana felt startled. When Cowley came back onto the phone he said, 'I've just instructed my men to come there now. Are you armed?'

'There's a pistol.'

'Place it outside the room, and leave the door to the room open. This is just for your own safety, Miss Molner. But please do what I ask.'

'Of course.'

'Goodbye, Miss Molner. For a while.'

The phone went dead. Diana stood, placed the heavy pistol outside the door and propped the door open with a chair. Then she went across to the window, pulled it up and leaned out, staring down at the street below.

Behind her, Rudi made disturbed sounds, but she ignored him now. If it was too late, it was too late; if it was not, then Rudi would be saved. Either way, there was nothing else she could do to help him.

Less than half a minute later the red car streaked round the corner, and pulled up with a squeal of brakes outside the Flora Hotel. Two men got out, one of them with dishevelled, curly hair, the other looking dark and sullen as he glanced up at the watching girl.

They ran into the hotel foyer. She could hear their footfall as they raced up the stairs.

She turned to face the door as the two of them ran lithely down the corridor. The sullen faced one picked up the gun and tucked it into his belt. The more boyish featured man gave her a quick smile, but entered the room with his pistol gripped between both hands, and extended before him as he turned to face all parts of the tiny quarters. When he was satisfied that there was just the girl, and the dying man, he relaxed.

He came over to her. 'Ray Doyle,' he said, 'CI5.' He flashed his ID card and she nodded. Roughly, then, he took her by the arms, turned her to face the wall and leant her against it, spreading her legs with a firm, if painless kick of his foot.

He frisked her thoroughly and intimately.

71

She was shaking as she turned back round in answer to Doyle's abrupt command. She was frightened. They seemed so young, yet they were so hard. They might do her damage.

But Doyle smiled, more lingeringly this time, and raised his hand in a gesture of peace. 'Don't worry love. It's all right, now. Everything's going to be all right.'

Cowley received word that the contact had been made, without violence, without casualties. He felt immensely relieved. The whole atmosphere in CI5 Control lightened. Cowley's concern for the well-being of the enigmatic Diana Molner had infected everyone in the room.

His relief was like a breath of fresh, breezy air.

The female controller called across to him. 'Re your requested contact with Somerfield, sir . . .'

'Ah, yes.' He walked over to her, rolling down his sleeves, getting ready to face the outside world again.

'I'm afraid Liaison denies all knowledge of anyone of that name.'

Damn, Cowley thought. *Always the block. Always the nervousness!*

'How far up did you get?'

The woman shrugged, and smiled. 'Well, as far as Assistant Control. I'd have thought . . .'

'You mentioned my name?' said Cowley, stung to think that the Department would have spoken to her from such a level and still denied him; perturbed at the way the girl had seemed to defend his feelings.

I'm not that crusty. Am I?

The woman nodded. 'I told him exactly who you were.'

Cowley was angry. He snapped at her, 'Then call him again. Repeat the request, and advise him that if I can't talk to Somerfield right away, then CI5 will issue an emergency internal requisition to interrogate.'

'Yes sir.'

Cowley moved away, shrugging on his jacket.

The grey car was parked down the street, about a hundred

yards from the Flora Hotel. The man who sat inside the undistinguished vehicle was smoking, staring thoughtfully at the ambulance that had parked on the pavement outside the hotel.

He started with surprise when the passenger door of his car opened and Joe Thomas slid into the seat. The man was sweating and unhappy. He carried a small case, and inside the case there was certainly a rifle, broken down into a number of parts.

'How many?' asked Thomas.

'Two. They're young. Hard. Look efficient.'

'How long've they been there?'

'CI5? About four, five minutes. The ambulance just came. You'd better hurry. I reckon from up there . . .' the man leaned forward and pointed through the windscreen to the flat-topped roof of the building opposite the Flora Hotel.

Thomas nodded. 'Be waiting for me.'

'Of course.'

Joe Thomas stepped from the car again and walked briskly along the street, vanishing between two buildings as he worked his way up to the best vantage point.

There were two shots to be fired. That meant getting a good, clear view.

Ray Doyle kept an eye on Diana Molner, simultaneously watching the street below – he couldn't see the grey car that had followed them earlier, and felt vaguely satisfied that they'd thrown the pursuer off. One less complication at the moment, even though they couldn't assume that they were not being watched, and that an assassination attempt was unlikely at the moment.

Doyle scanned the buildings opposite, checking every window, every ledge. The roofs were clear, sharp lines against the bright summer sky.

There was no obvious, covert movement.

Diana Molner remained calm and quiet, watching as the medical orderlies gently moved Rudi onto the stretcher, and rapidly assessed the state of his wound.

'I think we're too late,' one of them said.

Doyle said, 'What's wrong?' He cast a glance at Diana and saw that her eyes were closed. She was smoking a cigarette, the smoke rising in lazy wreaths above the smouldering tip. She had inhaled very little.

The medical attendant shook his head. 'He's lost too much blood.'

The second man rummaged in a haversack and produced a plastic blood bottle. He connected the fresh blood up to a needle and tube, and ran the needle quickly into one of the veins on Rudi's arm. He had difficulty finding the blood vessel and swore loudly.

Finally the drip was connected up, and Bodie took hold of it, watching impassively as the men worked on Rudiger Molner's unconscious body.

'We might be in time ... Lift!'

The two men raised Rudi's body on the stretcher. 'Keep that blood bottle high. It's a gravity feed.'

'Are you ready?' Doyle asked Diana, and the girl dropped the cigarette onto the floor, ground it out with her foot and nodded. As she moved away from the window, she stopped, stared searchingly at Ray Doyle.

'I don't suppose ...'

What did she want, Doyle wondered? There was something haunted about her. 'You don't suppose what?'

'The other man. Philip Latimer. He was almost ... almost dead when we brought him in .'

Now Doyle understood. 'I'm sorry,' he said. 'If you'd got him help sooner ...'

Diana nodded, her lips pinched together, her eyes lowered. 'Rudi wouldn't allow it.'

Doyle felt himself drawn to this beautiful and elegant, yet very vulnerable girl. She was not what he had expected at all, not the usual young female dealer in drugs. There was practically a stereotype for that particular brand of woman: dark glasses, mediterranean slacks for dress, a sense of wealthy confidence, but a strong sense of the mask that covered the rather shallow interior.

Diana Molner struck him as being deep, sensitive, a girl

who had been in touch with love, who was not self-obsessed.

He took her arm gently as he led her after the stretcher. She didn't flinch, seemed almost to move a little closer.

As they reached the foyer of the small hotel they all stopped. Bodie passed the blood bottle to Doyle, who again was told to hold the precious liquid higher. Diana walked to the front doors on Bodie's instruction. Bodie had stepped out, slightly onto the front steps. He scanned the road to east and west, then let his gaze flicker expertly up the various buildings opposite.

It all looked very quiet. The ambulance stood close by, its rear doors opened and ready to receive its passengers. Bodie turned back and beckoned to Diana Molner. He made her wait at the edge of the door itself. 'When I say go, you run to the ambulance and bundle in. Got it?'

'Got it,' she repeated thinly.

'Go!' said Bodie, after a further, cursory glance round. Diana Molner scampered past him, and he helped her on her way with a shove on the back that practically sent her sprawling.

'Come on!' Bodie called, and the medical orderlies came through the doors, bearing the weight of Rudi Molner. Doyle trotted beside them, holding the blood bottle high above the supine man's arm.

'Quickly!' Bodie urged.

They struggled to lift the stretcher into the back of the ambulance.

That was when the plastic bottle of blood shattered in Doyle's hand, blood splashing around, splattering his face and clothes. The gun shot sounded immediately after, coming from on high.

'Damn!' screamed Doyle, cupping the bottom of the plastic container, trying desperately to keep the blood that remained flowing into Rudi's veins.

Two more shots struck around him, one of them striking the ambulance and ricocheting with a great smash of glass through the hotel door.

The orderlies, and Bodie, tugged the stretcher into cover, practically flinging it onto the bed. A moment later the

75

ambulance lurched away, its rear doors swinging. Doyle leapt aboard and dragged the doors closed, but not before he had cast a last, searching stare back at the roofline, trying to see where those shots had come from.

He turned to see the state of things in the ambulance. One of the medics was stooped over Rudi, taking his pulse. Bodie sat grimly by, watching the procedure. Diana, after a moment, crawled round beside Rudi and put her arm around his head.

The medic straightened up and looked at her, then gave a little shrug of commiseration. Diana's gaze hardened, and she watched Doyle.

There was no warmth in her eyes.

Chapter Eight

The 'safe' house was a nondescript, semi-detached building in Islington, half way along a side-road between Upper Street and Essex Road. It had been in use by CI5, and indeed by MI5, for over seventeen years. Standing three storeys high, the lower floors had been converted into an ordinary, rather garishly furnished flat, and the operatives who maintained it both lived there, and communed easily with the neighbours.

Had any visitor attempted to mount the stairs to the first landing, however, he would have come across a door that was not a door.

The way to the 'safe' portion of the house was up a secret stairs, reached through the coal cellar.

CI5 maintained over twenty such safe places for political prisoners, or targetted persons, to be taken to. In the event of a siege each house could remain self-sufficient with six occupants for up to three months. At any one time only four or five houses were in use, their main occupancy being agents who needed, for a while, to keep a 'low profile', or criminals of the heavy cruiser class who had, even as long as a year ago, informed on their syndicate. Such men were evacuated from the country in no set way.

CI5 did not like to establish patterns.

The house behind Upper Street was George Cowley's favourite place for interrogation. As a younger man, still working for the Ministry of Defence and MI5, he had used the ground floor flat as his home; he had maintained the safe house with a 'friend'. It had been, in one sense, his first real home, since up until that time he had lived in smaller apartments wherever Whitehall had decided he should live.

He had, for a couple of years, been a part of the

community in that small sector of Islington, and still regarded it with fondness.

He parked his car some way from the house and met up with Bodie, strolling along the quiet street, affectionately remembering those earlier years. He was dressed more casually than usual, to avoid drawing too much attention to himself. Perversely, Bodie was wearing a natty, tailored suit, the white shirt open at the neck.

'All dressed up, Bodie ... and somewhere to go?'

Bodie smiled. 'I was hoping to snatch a little sleep later on.'

Cowley remembered the phone call that had summoned Bodie into Control. 'You sleep in your best suit?'

'The suit comes off,' murmured Bodie.

They reached the house. It had been repeatedly re-painted by its various occupants, and was now a tasteful cream, with brown window gloss. Cowley led the way down the steps at the front to the entrance in the small basement. They made appropriate sounds of greeting as the door was opened to them, and then made their way to the narrow stairs that led to the first landing.

Two CI5 men stood there, checked Cowley's ID, even though they knew full well who he was, then nodded him through.

On this first landing were the kitchens, store-rooms and bedroom cubicles. The interrogation room was on the top level, and Bodie trotted up the stairs, pushing into the small, breezy room.

As Cowley followed him in, shrugging off his jacket, Ray Doyle stood up. He had been sitting by the window, idly staring out through the heavy white netting; a copy of the Times, opened at the crossword, was spread out on his lap.

He had only managed five clues.

Diana Molner glanced up too. She was seated at the small table, a still-full cup of cold tea before her. She was cradling her head in her hands, staring at nothing. As she looked up Cowley could see that she had been crying.

He sat down opposite her, surveyed her for a moment, his strong face solemn; then he allowed himself to smile at her.

'I can understand that you are distraught, Miss Molner. But there are some questions that I have to ask you!'

She stared at him, her handsome features almost girlish in the way she was half pouting with sulkiness, and anger, and grief. She was recognising his voice from the phone, but wasn't quite sure.

Cowley said, 'I am George Cowley, head of CI5. Do you mind if I call you Diana?'

She said, 'It *is* you. *You* murdered my brother. You said you would protect us! You killed him!' Her eyes burned with hate; her face, so childlike a moment ago, took on the hard-edged look of a much older, much more experienced woman.

George Cowley just said, 'That is not true, Diana. You must believe me.'

'I trusted you!' she snapped back. '*Yours* was the voice I spoke to. *You* are the one who arranged it.'

'We did our best to save his life, and yours.'

She sneered contemptuously, eyes narrowed, hostile. 'Oh yes! Of course you did. That was just a charade, why don't you admit it? A piece of theatre to fool the world! But you don't fool me. I know how you do things in this country.'

Ray Doyle had been listening to the girl's anger with growing impatience, his handsome features scowling with irritation. Bodie had grinned at him and just shrugged. But now Doyle slapped his paper down onto the floor, walked across to lean on the table and said sharply, 'If that's the case, then why didn't we kill you too? And why shoot a blood bottle rather than the far easier target of the man on the stretcher?'

Diana shrugged, giving Doyle a withering look. 'How do I know the way your minds work? Maybe you did try. Maybe your man missed.'

Ray Doyle backed away, making a sound of exasperation.

But something had been nagging at him ever since the shooting. And it was the simple fact that the man behind the rifle *had* missed the body of Rudiger Molner. And yet his stray shot had burst the life-sustaining blood bottle.

One theory could read that the man had not been quite in

position when the group, of CI5 and the Molners, had emerged from the hotel. There was a second possibility. The assassin had not *wanted* to kill directly.

He had struck his target perfectly: the bottle of blood. He had hoped, perhaps, that death would then follow, and in that way he had been right.

Doyle felt the twinge in his shoulder where a girl called May Li had shot him twice, just those few months ago. He could still see the gaping mouth of the gun barrel pointed at his head, to administer the coup-de-grace.

The roar of the shot . . .

The splintering of wood and plaster as she aimed to miss, unable to kill so cold-bloodedly.

It was not unknown for even the hardest of agents to be unwilling, or unable, to commit the ultimate attack.

Bodie was saying, in answer to Diana's determined belief that it was CI5 who had killed Rudiger and Philip Latimer, 'Then why don't we kill you now?' He drew out his heavy duty Magnum and pointed it at her. 'If all we want is your death, I could take you out right now.'

'But you're not ready to,' she said sourly, facing the hand gun without flinching. 'You'll make it look like an accident. You're cowards.'

'But Diana,' insisted George Cowley, an edge of frustration in his normally controlled voice. 'Diana, why should we kill you?'

'For the same reason you killed Rudi!' she shouted, 'The same reason you killed Philip!'

'But what was that reason?' asked Cowley. 'What reason do you imagine we have for wanting you all dead?'

Ray Doyle said, 'Yeah. Come one, tell us. I'd like to know too, since I damn near got my head shot off outside the hotel.'

She looked from one to the other, confused, bewildered, miserable; only her defiance held her together, kept her abrasive.

'Why do you ask me these stupid questions?'

Cowley said, 'Because we want to know who killed your

brother, and Philip Latimer. We want to know who killed them, and why.'

'You can help us find out,' said Ray Doyle, softening slightly.

Bodie nodded his agreement, adding, 'You're the only one who can.'

She was momentarily cornered, quite helpless. The confusion in her face gave way to doubt. She was a woman who badly needed to trust someone, but whose training would not allow her to relax finally.

Wherever she came from, whichever country, it was clearly a most repressive place. The need for silence had been drilled into her.

She said, 'Who are you all? Why should I help you?'

'We are keepers of the peace,' said Cowley softly. 'We try to keep the streets safe for people, of whatever nationality, of whatever persuasion. Don't you want to know who killed your brother?'

Suddenly Diana's features hardened and she laughed, a light, cynical laugh, narrowed eyes glancing quickly, contemptuously at each man in the room. 'Now I see it!'

'Now you see what?' asked Cowley, sensing that an initiative had just been lost again.

Diana Molner said, 'This is how they do interrogations in my country too!'

'Really?' said Bodie, sounding bored.

'Really!' snapped Diana.

'And what country is that, exactly?' prompted Ray Doyle.

Diana shook her head slowly, her eyes narrowed with arrogant amusement. 'Oh no. I'm saying nothing. You're not tricking me with your clever techniques.'

Doyle exchanged a puzzled glance with Bodie. Clever techniques? The girl was so paranoid about interrogation that she'd be suspicious even of the question, Do you want another cup of coffee?

George Cowley said sharply, 'Where did the cocaine come from?'

'What cocaine?'

'How did you bring it into the country?' Cowley persisted, fixing Diana with a direct stare.

'*Did* you bring it into the country?' asked Doyle.

'Or was it manufactured here?'

Diana Molner said, 'What cocaine? I don't know what you're talking about.'

'The cocaine we found in Philip Latimer's apartment rooms,' said Cowley dully. 'The cocaine that caused an innocent girl to die, that led to the death of Philip Latimer himself. The cocaine that you left behind when you and your brother helped the dying Latimer from the house in Westbury Grove. The cocaine that looks and tastes like cocaine, and has the required effect when taken in whatever way you care to take it, but which isn't cocaine when you analyse it. Do you *now* remember what cocaine I'm talking about, Miss Molner?'

Cowley had talked hard, with heavy cynicism. The information had nevertheless blasted into Diana Molner, stirring up memory after memory. She looked shell-shocked, confused, and very shaken.

But she still said nothing.

Cowley went on, 'How did you intend to sell it?'

'Did they tell you who to take it to?' asked Bodie, leaning forward on the table.

Ray Doyle asked, 'Or were they going to leave it up to you?'

Diana suddenly erupted, frustration making her voice rise shrilly as she shook her head, eyes closed, to silence them. 'They! They! They! You're driving me crazy! Who the hell is "They"? I don't know any "They".'

Angrily, Bodie said, 'The ones you're fronting for. You know, the Big Fish, the guys with the money.'

'The ones who sent you here,' Cowley went on. 'The ones who funded Philip Latimer. The ones who can afford to buy, use and discard idealistic little kids like you.'

Ray Doyle came in, softer in tone, playing the good cop routine, even though he was sure that Diana would be aware of it. 'Look,' he said, 'Can't you see that you've been set up by ruthless people?'

'Who didn't give a thought about your brother's life,' added Bodie.

'Or,' said Cowley, leaning forward on the table and stabbing a finger at the girl, 'Or for the life of that poor girl who got killed, the innocent party in the whole affair.'

'Poor!' snapped Diana Molner, and this was a new emotion; not anger, nor defensiveness; it was a contempt of a different quality. It was almost patronising. 'Poor!' she repeated, and she looked at each man in turn, a withering, blistering gaze of pity at their appalling ignorance. 'What do any of you in this country know about poverty?' She laughed sourly.

Ray Doyle admired the way she had latched onto the single word, and changed its context and its meaning, avoiding the previous issue in order to gain the upper hand.

Cowley watched her impassively. She was, of course, beginning to crack; whatever she said next would give the beginnings of an insight into what made Diana Molner tick.

She said, 'Do you have starving peasants? Malnutrition? Children dying of tuberculosis and curable diseases?' Her voice was high pitched, harsh, a deeper anger informing her relationship with the three CI5 men now. 'Well? Do you? Do you have young people going blind through vitamin deficiency, because the money for medical research, and supplies, is reduced by ninety percent to line the pockets of the elite?'

Ray Doyle exchanged a curious glance with Bodie. Cowley just stared at Diana Molner, his arms folded, his eyes narrowed thoughtfully. 'Interesting,' he said quietly.

Diana Molner reacted with intense bitterness, practically shrieking at Cowley, 'Interesting! You find the third world *interesting*?'

Ray Doyle picked up her tea cup, and said almost innocently, 'Another cup of tea?'

Diana's face was red with anger. She glared at Cowley, then at Doyle, who was walking from the room.

Behind him, Cowley said softly, 'No, Miss Molner. I find *you* interesting.'

Ray Doyle closed the door behind him. In a way he was

glad to escape the atmosphere in the room. The girl had broken at last; Doyle's job was effectively done. For the future there might be a role in protecting her, then in going after any other members of her small group. But now Cowley would press home the advantage he had gained.

Once she had given an inch, she would give all the way.

And Doyle felt reluctant to watch the process by which so beautiful a girl, so self-possessed a girl, would have to adopt the role of informer, would have to betray herself in the face of overwhelming odds.

She had dealt in cocaine, and that made Doyle feel sick. But he had sensed her compassion; he had heard her tears when she had called from the Flora Hotel; he had touched the ordinariness in her, the woman who had regarded her brother as family, and not just as an agent of the revolution, a number, a cipher, to be obliterated without compassion when his job was done.

To Doyle, she was very real. If she had dealt with drugs then there was a very real reason for it, a reason beyond self promotion and profit.

As he trotted down the stairs to the kitchen, he supposed that he didn't want to wait around in the room and perhaps discover that he was wrong.

The kitchen was at the front of the house. As he filled the kettle with water, he glanced out of the window.

A car had pulled up outside the safe house. Three dark-suited men had stepped out and were obviously about to enter the basement.

Doyle quickly turned off the tap and raced upstairs. Cowley was standing behind Diana Molner, who looked pale, shocked, very vulnerable.

'Some funny men have arrived,' Doyle said from the doorway, and Cowley frowned, alarmed.

'Funny?'

'*Very* funny.'

George Cowley knew immediately what Doyle meant. He glanced at Bodie, indicating silently that Bodie should stand guard, then followed Doyle from the room.

They went downstairs to meet the unwelcome visitors.

Earlier, at about the time that Diana Molner was being brought into the 'safe' house, Raoul Northcott had played host to Colonel Eduardo Torres.

He had been seated behind his desk, reading the briefly scrawled report of the operative Joseph Thomas. Thomas had fired three rounds at the Molners, and succeeded in destroying the life support system of the boy, Rudiger.

He had missed the girl.

He had probably not even tried to hit her.

When the intercom buzzed to announce the arrival of Colonel Torres, Northcott straightened up, slid the piece of paper into his drawer, then stood to greet his visitor.

Torres was a squat, swarthy skinned man, looking every bit the South American military man he was. Dressed in a precisely trimmed dark suit, with a dark tie and so much grease on his hair that his head reflected the strip lighting above Northcott's desk, the man looked impeccably formal.

'Good to see you, Colonel,' said Northcott, as the two men shook hands.

'Greetings, Mr Northcott.' Torres looked unhappy, his eyes reflecting his nervousness at being asked to come to the Foreign Office of this strange land.

Northcott said simply, 'I'm afraid that CI5 have got hold of the Molner girl.'

And Eduardo Torres closed his eyes and exhaled sharply, his whole body seming to sag, reflecting the bitter disappointment, and deep sense of shock, that coursed through him.

He said, 'Then it is all over. I can hardly believe it. So much work – and now it is all finished.'

Northcott walked around the desk, reached a hand out to grip the older man's arm. He helped pull Torres back into the correct military bearing for such a man, back straight, face calm, able to look Northcott straight in the eye.

Northcott said, 'It's *not* all over, Colonel. Have courage. Have faith.'

'I have courage in plenty, Mr Northcott. I have little faith left in you.' It was a touch cold, but Northcott didn't mind that. He couldn't cope with defeatism. He could cope ably with criticism.

'The girl's brother is dead,' Northcott explained. 'The chemist is also dead. She is the only one left to worry about.'

Torres said sharply, 'But that is enough! They will make her talk!'

'She may talk, but what does she know? What does she really know? A scattering of facts. A scattering of names.'

Torres shook his head, still shocked, still convinced that everything was now finished. 'They will manage to piece it all together.'

Northcott said, 'Only if they question her for long enough! And she will resist for a long time.'

'What good is that? Long, short, if she tells what she knows, we are finished. We have no way out.'

'We can extricate legally,' said Northcott calmly.

'How?' asked the South American. His worry dissipated slightly, but he still looked anxious.

Northcott smiled, led Colonel Torres towards the door, picking up his coat as he went. 'By using International Law, Colonel. International Law.' He looked hard at Torres as he led the way from his offices. 'But you will have to play your part. And you will have to play it very carefully.'

They trotted down the steps from the Foreign Office building, picking up an agent called Powell on the way. A dark limousine was parked nearby and Northcott led Torres towards it.

'What exactly is my part?' the Colonel asked.

'I'll explain in the car,' Northcott said. 'The girl is being held at a not very safe 'safe' house. We know exactly where. Once there, you'll leave the talking to me, except for when I tell you to speak. Now listen . . .'

'How the hell did they find out about this house?' snapped Cowley, as he and Doyle waited on the first floor for the agent downstairs to usher the Foreign Office man up to him.

'Don't know, sir,' said Doyle. 'Perhaps we were followed? It was all happening so fast, we might have failed to notice a tail on us.'

Cowley eyed him angrily. 'Dammit, Doyle, this house has stood firm for seventeen years. The Department of Dirty Tricks should not have known about it.'

'Who knows what these Foreign Office boys tell each other,' said Doyle nonchalantly, and added, 'after lights out.'

George Cowley scowled at him. 'That's enough of that, Doyle.'

And then the two men entered the room, ushered in by a CI5 man who made a quick hand signal that said they were unarmed and had been so when they'd arrived.

The taller of the two men stepped up to Cowley and shook hands. 'Northcott. Foreign Office. You must be Cowley.'

'George Cowley. Correct. This is Ray Doyle.'

'Mr Doyle,' Northcott acknowledged, then turned to the dark skinned man behind him. 'May I introduce His Excellency Senor Eduardo Torres, Special Attache at the Embassy of the Government of General Olivares of Escondia.'

Torres took two quick steps forward, shook hands and clicked his heels. He regarded Cowley suspiciously, glanced at Doyle with disdain, then took two steps backwards.

So far so formal.

Cowley waited.

Torres took a deep breath and began to reel off what was patently a prepared speech. Northcott watched and listened calmly, coldly. Torres seemed nervous as he spoke.

'Her Majesty's Government has informed our Consulate that you have in your custody a Diana Molner who is one of our subjects.'

Cowley said nothing, nor gave any indication of the correctness or otherwise of that statement. Torres hesitated just long enough to establish that there would be no response and went on, 'Miss Molner is in the service of our country and is granted the full protection of diplomatic immunity. As co-signatory of the Geneva Convention we request and demand that you release her forthwith.'

As he finished speaking, so Torres clicked his heels again and bowed slightly.

George Cowley watched him implacably for a long moment, and an atmosphere of tense expectation developed in the room. Ray Doyle had to suppress his smile. Cowley was brilliant at keeping the edge.

He said at last, 'There seems to be some mistake. We do hold a Diana Molner here. We are holding her under the Special Powers (Terrorism) Act. We also have her passport which is West German, and which gives no indication that the owner is part of the Diplomatic Corps, and protected by diplomatic immunity.' He paused for a second, watching the play of anxiety and confusion in Torres' face. Then said sweetly, 'It is possible, I suppose, that there are two Diana Molners?'

Colonel Torres realised that he was being baited and straightened up, looking angrily at the CI5 man. He reached into his tunic pocket and drew out several folded papers. Without saying a word he passed them to Northcott who smiled and passed them to Cowley. Cowley unfolded the sheets and quickly read their contents.

Northcott said, 'As you can see, Diana Molner has dual nationality. Those credentials, countersigned by our own Government, provide her with the necessary status.'

'Dated today?' said Cowley with a half smile. He imagined that if he rubbed at the ink it might be induced to run. There had obviously been some frantic activity in the Foreign Office.

Northcott acknowledged that with a half smile and a slight nod of his head.

Cowley said, 'Excuse me, but I'd like to check with someone. May I take these papers a moment?'

'Certainly,' said Northcott. 'They are only duplicates.'

Leaving Doyle behind, Cowley walked quickly back to the interrogation room, where Diana Molner sat looking sulky and unhappy; Bodie was leaning against the wall, arms folded, looking very bored.

There was clearly no communication going on between them.

'Well, Miss Molner,' said Cowley, walking to the table. 'Whoever your backers are, they appear to be very highly placed.'

She frowned as she stared at him. 'What do you mean?'

Cowley handed her the papers from Torres' Embassy. 'A gentleman has arrived from your Embassy. That's the Escondian Embassy. He's a representative of your Government. That's the Government of General Olivares. You've been provided with Diplomatic status.'

Bodie sniggered. 'Aren't you the lucky one.'

But Diana wasn't lucky, and she knew it. She scanned the papers quickly, growing increasingly alarmed. Then she looked up at George Cowley, and the word he would have used for the expression on her face was: terrified.

'I don't understand,' she said. 'I'm nothing to do with their Government. I don't understand ...'

'Don't you?' Cowley remained cold, hard, fixing her with a steel-eyed gaze that she found she couldn't break.

Weakly, almost pathetically, she said, 'It's a trick.'

Cowley shrugged. 'Not on our part, Miss Molner.'

'A trick,' she repeated quietly, still staring at the papers. Her hands were shaking as she held them. She was deeply convincingly scared. 'They'll kill me. They'll get me to the Embassy and kill me.'

'Is yours the sort of Government that would condone such brutal action?' said Cowley gently.

Diana Molner, close to tears, shouted at him, 'You know damn well it is! This is a trick to get rid of me. You can't let them take me!'

'Better with them, with your own kind, than with us. I'm sure you'll be treated fairly.'

She looked shocked. She turned to look at Bodie whose smooth, dark features never flinched, never gave the slightest sign of what he was feeling. To Cowley she said, 'You must be mad. You can't believe that. I'm dead if you let me go. And I'm not ready for that.'

Cowley hesitated only briefly, then nodded his head and

walked over to her, almost dragging her to her feet. 'Come with me.'

He picked up the papers again and led Diana Molner roughly down the stairs and into the room where Northcott and Torres waited impatiently.

As Diana stepped into the room, Cowley could feel her body tense up. She had eyes only for Colonel Torres, and she was immediately afraid of him.

Torres took a step towards her and said, with a seriousness in his voice that was very artificial, 'Miss Molner. You and your brother were trafficking in illegal drugs. In order to prevent great shame and disgrace falling on our country, our Military Rulers have given you honorary diplomatic status.'

Diana Molner said nothing.

Raoul Northcott smiled at her. 'You don't seem very pleased, Miss Molner. The Foreign Office is prepared to accept the retroactive emendation, on condition that you are repatriated within twenty-four hours.'

'And what if I refuse?' demanded Diana, staring hard and defiantly at Colonel Torres.

Northcott just said, 'You cannot refuse.'

'I can claim political asylum!'

It was something that they had not thought of, in the haste with which they had left the Foreign Office with the newly prepared papers. Torres frowned fleetingly, alarmed at the prospect. Northcott inclined his head slightly, a gesture that was quite unreadable.

Diana looked wildly at George Cowley. 'Can't I? Can't I claim political asylum?'

George Cowley nodded. Behind him, Ray Doyle and Bodie watched the exchange with intense interest.

But Colonel Torres had an answer up his sleeve. He said softly, meaningfully, 'If you choose that course, Miss Molner, and *if* asylum is granted, you will bring international humiliation to your country – and possible retribution to your friends and relatives at home.'

It was like a punch to the solar plexus! It winded Diana,

the sting in the tail of Torres' little speech. There were too many friends at home, too many relatives. And she knew full well that the Government of General Olivares was quite capable of cold-blooded assassination, and very willing to carry out its blackmail threats.

Torres came up to her and put his hand on her arm, trying to be reassuring. He smelled of hair-grease and deodorant and Diana recoiled from him. His grip just increased, a painful pressure on her elbow.

He said, 'You must think not only of yourself. The consequences of any thoughtless action on your part could be very wide reaching.'

'Bastard,' Diana Molner whispered, and Torres smiled. 'Will you come?'

'I have no choice.'

She let Torres guide her gently towards the door. Behind them Northcott smiled with satisfaction, looked round at the grouped CI5 men, and shrugged slightly. It was a posturing arrogance that made Cowley's skin crawl. But Cowley himself had a card left to play, and he said sharply, 'A moment, if you please, Colonel Torres . . .'

Diana Molner's sudden look at George Cowley was a reaffirmation of the fear she felt at being taken by representatives of her Government; her eyes radiated a desperate hope. She was practically pleading with him to do something.

Eduardo Torres looked apprehensive, slightly angry. He hesitated by the door, conscious that Ray Doyle had moved towards him, a vaguely menacing gesture.

Cowley went up to Diana and placed his hand gently on her shoulder. 'Diana Molner, I hereby arrest you, and charge you with being an accessory to murder and conspiracy to trafficking in drugs.'

He turned to Northcott. 'Until Miss Molner's diplomatic status has been legally acknowledged in a magistrate's court, she will remain officially under the care and custody of CI5.'

Colonel Torres' face darkened with frustration and anger. He looked sharply at Raoul Northcott. 'What does this mean? I thought all this had been worked out!'

Northcott shrugged wearily. 'It's a tiresome formality, Colonel. But a formality it is.'

George Cowley smiled thinly as he said, 'Like your own Government I'm sure, Colonel, I am quite a stickler for detail. If something is to be done, it must be done correctly. I'm sure you would have it no other way.'

Torres sagged, shaking his head. Northcott said, 'Fine. If we're now all agreed, perhaps we may proceed?'

'We are not standing in your way,' said Cowley.

They all left the safe house, gathering on the pavement outside, between the limousine that belonged to the Foreign Office, and Ray Doyle's car, which another agent had driven from its parked place some way away.

'Will you ride with us, Miss Molner?' asked Colonel Torres, but before Diana could reply, Bodie had placed himself between the girl and the Government man. He shook his head and smiled.

'She goes with us,' he said.

'Very well,' said Northcott, with an easy shrug. He led Colonel Torres to the limousine and climbed in. He immediately picked up the car phone and began to speak, and that simple action, observed by George Cowley, sent a shiver of anticipation down the CI5 Chief's spine.

What the hell was going on?

Kids running cocaine. The Department of Dirty Tricks, attached to the Foreign Office, in league with the Military Government of a country with which Britain had very poor relations . . .

Cowley had too many questions for the sparsity of answers that he was receiving.

He needed Somerfield. Damn Somerfield for playing so hard to get!

Bodie and Ray Doyle bundled Diana Molner into their car and slid off in pursuit of the limousine. They would go straight to the Magistrate's Court, and the legal operation, to acknowledge Diana's diplomatic status, would take no more than an hour.

It was very little time!

Cowley walked back to his own car, face grim. He was so deep in thought that he forgot to cast a last, nostalgic glance back at a safe house that would now have to be abandoned by CI5.

Chapter Nine

Doyle pulled up outside the imposing facade of the Magistrate's Court, immediately behind Northcott's limousine.

Colonel Torres and the Foreign Office man were already standing at the front entrance, hands in pockets, waiting for Diana Molner to be delivered to them. A CI5 agent called Middleton was waiting there, ready to stand guard at the front entrance. While Doyle watched, so the lawyer who would be representing Colonel Torres' request joined them.

Diana Molner watched the group, her face pale, her hands shaking. 'I'm frightened,' she said.

Ray Doyle leaned over the back of the driver's seat, not smiling, but regarding the girl with gentleness. 'You played with fire. People who play with fire shouldn't be frightened.'

'But I am. My brother is dead. My lover is dead. If I were dead then a very great problem would be resolved.' She stared at Ray Doyle; her eyes were wide, beautiful, warm. She was calm, now, despite the fear she felt. She said, unexpectedly, 'You don't like me very much, do you, Mr. Doyle?'

Bodie half turned, glancing at his companion, then looked back to where the group by the entrance to the Courts were getting restless.

'I don't like what you represent,' Doyle said. 'I find it abhorrent.'

'Dealing in drugs, you mean.'

'Dealing in human weakness.'

She smiled thinly, but not patronisingly. 'Mr Doyle, where I come from, it is human weakness itself that is the commodity to be bought and sold. I find it abhorrent too. I wish you could understand.' She began to open the door to the car. 'Sometimes it is necessary to fight fire with fire.'

She got out of the car and walked elegantly and steadily towards Torres. Bodie watched her go. 'Speaks good English. Very good English.'

Doyle said, 'Not at all your usual drug dealer.'

'Or even terrorist.'

'So what is she?' Doyle shook his head in answer to his own question.

'More than she seems,' said Bodie, as he settled back to wait for the hearing to finish.

When George Cowley arrived back at his car he used the car phone to call CI5 Control. 'Anything on Somerfield?'

'I've been trying to contact you, sir,' came the voice of the controller. 'Somerfield has come out of the woodwork.'

'At last!' said Cowley, and breathed a deep sigh of relief.

Fifteen minutes later he was pulling off the road into an underground car-park, bouncing down the ramp, headlights on. It was a dark, fairly crowded place. He toured gently around the parked cars until he found a space, and tucked his own vehicle neatly in.

Headlights off, he left the car and walked towards the lift to the upper levels.

Standing close by, half concealed by shadow, was a thin, pale-faced man, his features gaunt, almost corpse-like. He was dressed in a dark suit, and smoking a cigarette. As Cowley approached he stepped forward a little, and extended his hand.

The palm was clammy, the grip weak. The man reminded Cowley of a middle-aged junkie, trembling, darting-eyed, moist lipped.

This was Richard Somerfield.

'I'm afraid nobody can help you very much with this man Northcott. Sorry, old boy.'

'Why is that?' asked Cowley quietly.

'His department is one of those funny ones,' said Somerfield. 'It has complete autonomy. Tends to breed little Hitlers, you know the sort of thing old boy. Dislikeable bunch.'

'A P.M. appointment?' Cowley asked, and Somerfield reacted with astonishment.

'Good Lord no! Ministerial awareness? Heaven forbid. As like as not the P.M. would disband it the moment she knew about its existence. Come on, George, you know the Civil Service. Got to protect the moral consciences of the people's representatives. Only tell 'em what they need and want to know.'

Cowley grunted his disapproval. 'Let's not open that particular can of worms. It's bad enough that I have to spend several hours getting *you* to acknowledge your existence.'

'Sorry George. You know how it is. Had to be sure that it was really important. Can't go disclosing facts about secret departments on every Home Office whim.'

'For your information, Richard,' said Cowley stiffly, 'I have no room in my work – or private life – for whimsy.'

'Point taken, old boy. Point taken.'

It was cold in the car-park's basement. Richard Somerfield was shivering violently, almost unable to get the cigarette into his mouth at times. His eyes gleamed in the sparse light from the entrance.

If this was what being in charge of Security Liaison did to you, Cowley thought, it made him glad to work even with the likes of Bodie and Doyle.

He said, 'If the P.M. doesn't know about the Department, then how is it answerable?'

'Usual channels,' said Somerfield crisply. He coughed on the smoke, then added, 'Usual long, exhaustive process. Official Complaint. Sub-committee. Closed hearings, and so forth.'

'By which time it's always too late.' Cowley observed, allowing the cynicism to richly lace his tone of voice.

Richard Somerfield could have cared very little less for the consequences of such Civil Service covert activity. 'The Diana Molner business,' he said, 'Is an entirely different – what can I say – kettle of fish? Or perhaps, can of worms?'

'Try nest of vipers,' said Cowley.

'You really are much too moral, George,' said Somerfield,

for the first time asserting himself and sounding a little perturbed at Cowley's defiance of normal Civil Service practice. 'If it wasn't for your threat of an emergency requisition I should have preferred to spare you some seamy details of the barely forgiveable face of secret diplomacy.'

George Cowley let his disapproval register in the sour little laugh with which he greeted that statement from Somerfield. 'Don't worry. I've looked under stones before. I know the things that crawl there.'

If Richard Somerfield would have loved to have mixed it with Cowley, he restrained himself, drew on his cigarette then threw the butt onto the ground. 'Miss Molner's father is highly placed in the right wing military junta in her country.'

'Ahhh,' said Cowley, as things began to slot into place.

Somerfield went on. 'We're talking about Escondia, of course.'

'Escondia being the cover name for a much more familiar country.'

'Of course. The country whose name we dare not speak. I'm impressed with you George, figuring that one out.'

'Oh come on, Richard, the F.O.'s little name games are well enough known.'

Somerfield nodded thoughtfully. 'Their country is completely broke. They're not alone in that, of course, but because of the current obsession with human rights in the world, and because of its fairly excessive record in that particular field, Escondia is having difficulty in finding trading partners and international loans.'

'I'm not surprised,' said Cowley.

Somerfield went on, 'Its biggest single source of income is . . . er . . .'

Cowley merely shrugged. 'Cocaine, of course.'

'Of course,' said Somerfield evenly. 'It's remarkable how much help a single international loan can have on the survival of a country; or trade concessions, helping boost exports. But when the world turns its official back on you, there are always the unofficial trade mechanisms. It's rather funny to think that the very countries that have refused

97

International Monetary help have made their token apology by increasing their trade with Escondia in cocaine.'

'Funny?' echoed Cowley. 'You have a strange sense of humour, Richard.'

'I have no sense of humour at all, George. You ought to know that.'

Cowley said, 'So Escondia is very big in the world of cocaine?'

'Always has been. Home grown, and a terrific smuggling trade from neighbouring countries too, countries where the trade is officially repressed. And like all its more legitimate predecessors, the Olivares' Government has taken over the cocaine trade. It's virtually their only income, but it's worth eight hundred million pounds a year.'

Which didn't sound a great deal, until one realised that the country in question was a typical Military-run dictatorship, with a massive peasant population at little better than starvation level, and an elite of families whose riches were not dependent upon their country's prosperity at all, but on wealth accumulated world wide. Their taxes would boost the Government's revenue, without making much of a dent in the life-style of the villa-mafiosi.

In most South American countries, such illicit trade as drugs was usually firmly in the hands of such families. In Escondia the families were the Government, and the Government was the Military. It was a country sewn up tighter than the British Foreign Office. Everyone benefited from the trade in cocaine.

Except the population, of course.

And suddenly George Cowley felt sick, sick for what Diana Molner had been doing on behalf of that Government, outletting their drug produce in London, probably supplying half of Western Europe. He said, the disillusion with Diana heavy in his voice, 'So the Molner girl was fronting that operation for them. Her and her brother.'

Somerfield laughed humourlessly, more in surprise than anything. 'The Molner girl? Good God no! Oh George, you have misunderstood!'

'Then what?'

'Diana Molner is further left than Trotsky! So was her brother Rudiger. They were trying to *stop* the drug trade from their country.'

Puzzled, Cowley said, 'To stop it? By selling several kilos of the stuff?'

Somerfield started to walk away from the lifts, Cowley pacing easily along next to him. 'What she tried to do was rather clever. The world cocaine centre has been shifting to London, as you probably know. So the Olivares' Government's main income now comes from here. Diana Molner found a research chemist called Philip Latimer who had figured out how to manufacture cocaine artificially in this country. Latimer had met Diana Molner about two years before and hinted that he'd figured out how to make the stuff artificially. Their relationship developed and we believe she fell in love with him. Quite naturally, and without subversive intent. Then what she and her fellow revolutionaries had to do was to cut in on the imported supply from her own country, replace it with their home-made stuff, and thus topple the dictatorship back home by strangling its funds.'

Cowley understood very clearly, now. Strangely, he felt a touch of relief at knowing the motive behind Diana Molner's actions, even though her actions would have added to the already horrendously large market for drugs in Western Europe.

'Then they ran into Northcott's department,' he said.

'Indeed,' said Somerfield. 'The Dirty Tricks boys. The trouble is, George, that Britain doesn't want Olivares' Government to fall, even though it's corrupt. Our policy is to sustain it.'

'Good God, why? What the hell for?'

'I'm not an oracle, George. I can't answer everything you ask.'

'But why not sustain the country officially, then? By sending foreign aid, for example?'

Somerfield smiled, raised a hand, one finger extended, as if he were lecturing. 'Because, officially, we are in favour of a return to democracy in that country, and we don't want to lose our trade agreements with her neighbours – which would certainly happen if we were found out to be supporting Olivares.'

'Diplomacy!' snapped Cowley. 'By God, it *is* a game.' He looked quizzically at Somerfield. 'So what happens to Diana Molner now?'

'I understand that she's being taken to court this afternoon. Her new diplomatic credentials will be presented. Then she'll walk out of the building and everyone's hands will be clean.'

'Including Northcott's?'

Somerfield laughed, getting Cowley's point. 'Yes, I suppose you've got a much cleaner job keeping the domestic house in order, haven't you George?'

They shook hands. Cowley went back to his car, drove out of the car-park and called Doyle.

Ray Doyle almost jumped out of his skin as the R/T sounded; he had been drifting off to sleep, not helped by Bodie's drowsy presence beside him.

The CI5 man Middleton was still at his station outside the court-house.

Answering the call, Doyle was not surprised to hear Cowley's deep voice. 'Has she come out yet?'

'Not yet. Seems to be dragging on.'

'Well things won't drag on much longer. I've had contact with Security Liaison. A very interesting chat. You're sounding sleepy, Four-five, so brighten up. There could be an attempt to assassinate Diana Molner as she leaves the court.'

That certainly did bring both Doyle and Bodie to full alertness. As he spoke to Cowley, so Doyle peered through the car's windscreen, scanning the streets and houses as he had done once before, looking for the tell-tale signs of covert activity.

Bodie checked backwards along the street, eyes narrowed as he studied each parked car.

'Listen carefully,' said Cowley. 'Anticipate strong resistance. Prevent danger to Diana Molner at all costs. I suggest you take her to maximum security as soon as she comes out. Have you got that?'

Doyle said, 'Four-five. Roger.'

'Understood.' Bodie.

'One more thing,' Cowley went on. 'This is now an Operation Susie. Over.'

Doyle exchanged an apprehensive glance with Bodie. 'Repeat that, Alpha One. Please.'

'The protection of Diana Molner is now an Operation Susie. Is that clear? Over.'

'Four-five. Operation Susie. Understood.'

Cowley's voice was softer than usual, as if he regretted the necessity of doing what he was doing. 'If anything goes wrong you are on your own. Abandon your identification and R/T. If *anything* goes wrong, you are on your own. This order will be erased. I will contact further. Good luck. Stand by.'

There was a pause. Doyle imagined that Cowley was talking to someone at the other end. The two of them sat quietly, apprehensively, staring at the court-house.

Then Cowley again, 'This is Alpha One to agents Three-seven and Four-five, on Operation Susie. You are as of now suspended for all active duties. Confirm and Return to Base. Over.'

Bodie clicked on his own R/T. 'Suspension confirmed, over and out.' Doyle repeated that response.

And that was that.

They emptied their pockets of ID cards, their wallets, and anything else they carried that might have been able to link them to CI5. Bodie locked them, and their R/T transmitters, into the glove compartment of the car.

'Park back down the road a way. We'll pick a car from that row by the houses.'

Doyle said, 'Are we doing this because we love him, or our jobs?'

With a grin, Bodie shook his head. 'What's the matter? Looking for some extra motivation?'

'We can't all be Hamlet,' muttered Doyle.

He drove the car in a U-turn and parked some hundred

yards away from their first station. It was a slightly unnerving feeling, to be out of contact with Control, to realise that they were now quite on their own. Whatever they did, the consequences of their actions were their own.

Bodie came up with extra motivation, to power the task before them.

'Rescuing a damsel in distress,' he said brightly. 'How about that? She's certainly a damsel, and she's certainly in distress.'

'Aren't you supposed to be in love with the woman?' Doyle added cynically.

'Work on it,' Bodie urged.

'Aren't damsels supposed to be young, innocent, vulnerable?'

'She's young,' Bodie agreed. 'But you can't have everything. Besides, we're no knights on white chargers.'

'Peasants with a smoke bomb,' added Doyle, and they exchanged a meaningful glance.

'What a good idea,' said Bodie.

They got out of the car and looked around. Bodie opened the boot and the two of them peered into the various boxes of equipment that were stuffed into the luggage space. Doyle picked up a small, silver cannister.

There was a fair bit of activity around them. The sun was bright, the day quite still.

'Visibility's good,' Doyle said.

'Got this funny feeling there's afternoon fog due.'

'It's a chance. We'd have to move fast.'

'But if Cowley's right, they'll be making a strike at her as she leaves the court.'

Doyle glanced at his wristwatch. 'Talking of which.' He glanced around at the various cars scattered along the sides of the road. 'Ford Cortina?'

'Don't like the steering,' said Bodie. 'How about a Rover 2000?'

'I'm not travelling in anything that looks so much like a Citroën. Had a Citroën once. Nearly killed me in repair bills. What about ...'

'What about something foreign?' Bodie promted, indicating a Lancia close by. He rattled his keys impatiently, and Doyle grinned and nodded.

'Why not?'

The simple legal process was over. It had taken a frustratingly long time, in Colonel Torres' estimation; an hour or more for something that in his country would have been achieved in a minute.

Throughout it all Diana Molner had remained silent, morose, deeply dejected. She had not responded to Torres' occasional reassuring smile. She half sensed what was in store for her.

They walked from the court, Torres with his hand on Diana's arm, Raoul Northcott on her other side and the lawyer behind them. In the foyer to the courthouse they hesitated.

Northcott said, 'We'll leave by the back entrance. It's a little safer.'

'Very well,' said Eduardo Torres, then to Diana. 'Welcome to the diplomatic community, Miss Molner.' He handed her her new passport and smiled.

She took the passport and stared down at it. She was pale and confused. She suddenly wanted Cowley around, or somebody, *any*body, whose declared interest was her well-being.

'What happens now?' she asked.

Northcott said, 'We suggest that you leave the country within twenty-four hours.'

'Otherwise you will be formally deported,' added Torres solemnly.

'In which case,' Northcott pointed out, 'You will be returned directly to your country.'

She was so confused. The diplomatic passport enabled her to visit many countries, and to settle under the wing of the Esconian embassy in that country. It all, suddenly, seemed very co-operative.

So why did she have a deep-rooted suspicion that this was all a trick? That things were not as they seemed?

'May I call my father from the Consulate?'

'It would be unwise,' said Torres, slightly apologetically. 'Come along, Miss Molner,' and he led her towards the rear exit from the courts.

'Here they come,' said Ray Doyle.

He and Bodie had just moved rapidly around the court-house, realising that the party was not leaving by the front entrance. It was the limousine that had given the change of plan away. It had moved sleekly away from its parked position some minutes before, and had suddenly turned up again along the side-road behind the building.

Bodie glanced quickly around. There were houses opposite, and a block of high-rise flats in the distance, from which a sniper might be able to make a single, good shot. There were also several trees in a small park, whose densely packed flower beds would have given good cover.

Ray Doyle ignited the smoke bomb and hurled it towards the steps leading down from the rear entrance. Bodie revved up the Lancia, already familiar and comfortable with the new car.

It all happened very quickly, then. The party appeared on the steps and watched, puzzled, as the dense white fumes from the smoke bomb billowed up before them. A car was racing towards them ...

Torres put a protective arm around Diana Molner, then seemed to grasp what was going on and jerked away from her, leaving her standing alone and exposed on the top step.

Two shots rang out. Glass shattered. Diana Molner screamed, crouching slightly, her hands by her head.

A third shot and she span backwards, hitting the wall of the court-house, sobbing loudly; then she lurched away, stumbling down the steps, her right arm bloody and dangling by her body. She stumbled into the smoke. Northcott yelled to her, but she couldn't hear him over her screams, and the roar of the Lancia which was braking to a halt next to her. Doyle jumped out and bundled the wounded girl into the back seat, and almost before he himself had climbed in, the car had roared away, Bodie spinning the wheel frantically, and screeching along the road.

Behind them, the smoke cleared slightly. Raoul Northcott glared into the distance, his face a mask of rigid anger. Colonel Torres looked bemused, then irritated, but Northcott brushed him off as he walked towards the waiting car and snatched up the phone.

Chapter Ten

George Cowley entered the computer room, glanced quickly around at the bustle of activity, then glanced anxiously at his watch.

If he smiled, then, it was an ironic little smile: here he was, anxious to hear from Bodie and Doyle, despite the fact that the two operatives were now suspended from active duty, and acting on their own initiative.

There would be no news from Four-five or Three-seven. Cowley would have to sweat it out.

The controller called over to him, confirming what Cowley already knew at a gut level:

'Foreign female diplomat has been abducted from Harvey Street Court-house by two men last seen approaching sector four on Bodlian Street from the east.'

'I see,' said Cowley. He was slightly relieved that someone, somewhere, was still able to monitor the abduction. Perhaps his worry was needless. Perhaps they wouldn't be shooting quite so much into the dark as he'd thought.

He asked, 'Have you located the Minister yet?'

'He's still in conference, sir. The Security Cabinet. Will the private secretary do?'

Cowley shook his head. He was impatient, apprehensive. He was playing for time, and time was at a premium. There would be a limited time-span during which Bodie and Doyle could get Diana Molner out of harm's way.

Until he saw the Minister, the girl was in danger. Deadly danger. Only the Minister could help. Only the Minister could call a halt to the merciless hunting of Diana Molner.

Or could he? George Cowley wasn't even sure on that point. But it was his only card left to play.

Unless . . .

He stared vacantly at the wall in front of him, and the glimmer of an idea began to form in his mind.

'There! Over there!'

Bodie span the wheel of the car. The Lancia churned up dust and gravel as it swung through more than ninety degrees, in through the open, broken gates of a disused factory yard. Bodie drove fast, searching for a way through the façade of decaying warehouses, away from the eyes of those who might be following.

At last he saw a door, gaping open, and took the car into the darkness within.

They ran through the heavy stillness, their footfalls echoing in the voluminous space of the warehouse. They found the small office at the back of the unit, an affair of prefabricated wooden partitions and concrete struts. The office was raised about twenty feet from the factory floor, overlooking the ground space.

It was defensible. Just.

The priority was to tend to Diana Molner's gunshot wound.

They crouched in the half light, listening to the silence outside. Bodie fumbled for a dressing from the small first aid pack he had taken from the Capri. He had counted on 'casualties', and was only glad that the casualty was so slight. 'Nothing serious,' he said to Diana, as he attended to the flesh wound. 'Hurt much?'

'Yes,' she said. 'I thought I was going to die.'

'Not from this,' said Bodie. 'Missed the bone, missed everything vital.'

Doyle was standing by the office window, staring anxiously across the warehouse, deep in thought.

Diana asked, 'What happens now?' Her voice was tremulous, nervous. She stared at Ray Doyle's back, then turned hollow, frightened eyes on Bodie.

Bodie shrugged. He didn't have an answer to that question.

And nor did Ray Doyle. 'Wish I knew, love. But we're on our own, now. I just hope,' he glanced round at Bodie, 'I just hope there's a guardian angel watching over us.'

Diana Molner was close to tears, shaking very badly. She was desperately confused, shocked by the gunshot wound.

'You rescued me. Whose side are you on?'

'I thought we'd got that clear,' said Doyle irritably. 'We're on your side.'

'The side of all damsels in distress,' added Bodie.

She shook her head. 'I don't understand.'

Ray Doyle came over to crouch by her. He put his arm round her shoulders and gave her a friendly hug. Bodie smiled sweetly at him, and Doyle narrowed his eyes impatiently: don't interfere!

'Look, love. We're just carrying out orders, and those orders are to protect you, against whoever is out there, and if necessary to defend you with our lives.'

She thought about that, tearfully regarding Doyle, then giving him a faint smile. 'Are we safe now?'

Bodie said, 'Don't worry, love. There's only one other person in the world who knows we've come here.'

'And he's on our side too,' added Ray Doyle.

Diana looked up. 'Mr Cowley?'

Bodie said, 'The very same.' He glanced at Doyle, a slightly worried look. Cowley *would* have guessed that they'd bring her here? They hadn't exactly had a good chance to talk plans before the Operation Susie had gone into action. Doyle had vaguely remembered this place from a previous assignment, and had vaguely hinted to Cowley that the abandoned factory complex might make a good hiding place.

Diana Molner was saying. 'He ... he makes people trust him. I like him.'

Exchanging amused glances, Doyle said, 'I think she has his number.'

'You hope,' added Bodie.

A CI5 lawyer called John Deville came to collect Cowley from the computer room.

'Fat's in the fire, George. Northcott's here. Time has run out for you.'

'Damn,' said Cowley, fetching his jacket. Deville was a young, instense looking man. Cowley had complete faith in him. 'Nothing we can do? No option?'

Deville shook his head. 'I've gone over it with the Attorney General's office. There's no position we can take at all. We have to comply with whatever they request.'

They left the computer room and met Raoul Northcott and his legal aide in a small reception room. Northcott was furious, but biting back that anger, so that only his white, thin lips and furrowed brow told of his deeply felt irritation with CI5.

Cowley ignored the formalities. 'Well?'

'Our information,' said Northcott bitterly, 'Is that two of your men, Bodie and Doyle, have kidnapped Diana Molner. Miss Molner has diplomatic status. If it is true that your men have abducted the woman, then according to the terms of the act under which CI5 was authorised as a Home Office Department, you must disclose their whereabouts, if known to you.'

Cowley said nothing, staring Northcott out until at last the Foreign Office man was forced to add, 'Refusal to do this could constitute treason. Technically. The penalties of which are well known to you.'

'I see,' said Cowley stiffly. 'Would you excuse me, for a moment?'

He walked across the room with Deville. The young lawyer was very agitated. He spoke in a low murmur as he said, 'We must comply!'

George Cowley reminded him that, 'The computer recorded the suspensions of duty of agents Three-seven and Four-five from *before* the time of abduction.'

'Meaningless,' said Deville.

'Supposing I don't know where they are?'

Deville said insistently, 'If Bodie and Doyle are found on our property, or at any subsequent time are found to have used CI5 property during the abduction, that will give them all they need to hang us. They'll eventually trace that smoke-bomb!'

'Yes. I'd thought of that.'

'So we must co-operate fully. Now,' said Deville, the urgency in his voice causing it to rise in volume slightly. Northcott watched them from across the room, looking smug.

'Can't we delay?' asked Cowley, clutching at straws.

'That is non-co-operation,' said the lawyer. 'In fact, it's worse. It's obstruction.'

Cowley hesitated again.

Deville added, 'Bodie and Doyle are finished anyway. Don't let them bring us down with them!'

Cowley said, 'But why does Northcott want her so badly?'

Deville just shrugged. 'I am sure that's something we would be better off not knowing.'

That strongly defensive statement from Deville took Cowley by surprise, and he gave the young legal expert a quick, searching look.

Perhaps John Deville wasn't quite as dependable as Cowley had thought.

Nevertheless, Cowley was forced to accept that Deville was right about the need to comply with the Foreign Office's demands. He returned to Northcott.

'The two former agents you have enquired about had access to all our safe houses, the lists of which are in your own computer. There are also safe houses that shouldn't be in your computer, but which I imagine you have managed to unearth.'

Northcott smiled humourlessly.

Cowley went on, 'In addition there is an emergency grounding station, special to the agents in question.'

It galled him to do this! It would put tremendous pressure on Bodie and Doyle. He only hoped they would understand. Thank God he had a final card up his sleeve, a last, desperate gambit.

'The ground station is a warehouse.'

He gave the address.

Northcott executed a little bow, flashed a triumphant smile. 'Thank you, Mr Cowley. You co-operation is appreciated.'

He turned to leave, but Cowley called after him.

'Northcott! The two agents in question are quite proficient. I suggest that in order to reduce casualties you give them every chance to surrender.'

Northcott said quietly, 'But of course, Mr Cowley. Of course.'

In the warehouse, seated on the floor of the deserted office, the three of them talked. Diana Molner had loosened up, become very talkative, almost relieved that at last she could trust someone. She stared mostly at Ray Doyle, perhaps still slightly frightened of Bodie's smooth, solemn good looks. Her arm was hurting like hell, but the pain was well diminished by the sense that at last she could talk her heart out.

She had lost everything there was to lose, except her life. Now was the time to start thinking of her personal future. She had done everything she could for the people of her country.

Now she was on her own, and she had to think of herself.

Ray Doyle was saying, 'If you and your brother had succeeded in selling that cocaine, what were you going to do with the money?'

'Buy weapons,' she said simply.

'Weapons for whom?' asked Bodie. This was a new twist, and he could see that Doyle was as puzzled by that answer as he was.

'For the resistance movement, of course,' said Diana Molner, as if nothing could have been more obvious.

'In your home country,' said Doyle unnecessarily, and Diana Molner wearily affirmed, not bothering to make a sarcastic comment.

Bodie said, 'But you hadn't actually bought any yet?'

'No.'

'Did they know what you had planned? The resistance people back home? Or were you and Rudiger acting on your own?'

'We were on our own,' said Diana. 'The resistance didn't trust us. Our father is Alexander Molner. He's in the military . . .'

111

Before she could say more, Ray Doyle cut in.

'Wait a moment. None of this is relevant any more. The point is ... the point is,' he repeated, more emphatically, stabbing a finger towards Diana, 'Diana here has been stopped from selling the cocaine. The only chemist who could make it is dead.' He looked towards Bodie. 'So why the hell are they still trying to kill her?'

'And trying so hard!' Bodie added.

'Even over our dead bodies.'

He turned back to Diana. 'Why were you such a threat to them? Why you? What is it you know that makes you so dangerous?'

But Diana Molner just shook her head; her ignorance was convincing.

She really didn't know.

If she had been intending to give voice to that lack of knowledge, she never got the chance, for at that moment a shot rang out from the dark warehouse area, shattering the window of the prefabricated office.

'Christ!' yelled Bodie, as the three of them flung themselves flat.

'So soon!' said Doyle, drawing his pistol and clicking off the safety.

Diana Molner panicked. Her voice was almost a scream as she cried out, 'I thought you said nobody but Cowley knew we were here!'

Doyle peered over the window sill. There was furtive movement on the ground floor below, especially towards the entrance to the factory space.

'Northcott's men,' he said.

Behind him, Bodie was rapidly assembling a rifle. He should have done this minutes before, but they had been too intent on Diana.

'How did they find us?' Diana wailed. A second shot crashed through the office, making Doyle duck quickly.

Doyle said, 'There's two outside.'

'Two more behind that concrete support,' said Bodie.

Diana went on, her voice a sob, 'Your Cowley! Your Mr

112

Cowley must have told them! I trusted him!'

Bodie ignored her. He was more concerned with estimating the danger represented by the new arrivals. Coolly, to Doyle, he said, 'A tactical withdrawal?'

'Tactical? Or strategic?' answered Doyle.

Bodie laughed cynically. 'Do we have a strategy?'

'We can delay them.'

Bodie pointed out that, 'Delay without reinforcements – that's tactics.'

'Our only tactic.'

A third shot ricocheted off the ceiling, making Diana scream and duck as plaster and wood showered down.

'Okay,' said Doyle. 'The roof.'

Ray Doyle bobbed up from behind the wall of the office and pumped shots frantically across the warehouse, to the two positions where he could see Northcott's men.

Concrete exploded, dust flew, the sound of the shots echoed and reverberated thunderously in the factory space. There was a spattering of answering fire, and Doyle ducked, listening to the whine of the rounds.

Behind him, Bodie hustled the girl out of the back door of the small office, along a catwalk to the skylight to the roof.

When they were safely out of sight, Doyle pumped three quick shots at the man he could see slightly exposed behind a concrete pillar, and when the shape darted into cover he turned and followed the other two onto the roof.

They crouched behind a cluster of chimneys, Bodie guarding the rear, Doyle watching the skylight. Diana crouched, trembling, between them.

'How's your arm?' asked Bodie.

'OK,' she said. 'It doesn't seem important suddenly.'

Doyle said, 'They want her dead. They wanted all of them dead. In a hurry too. Maybe that was it. Maybe that's the question! Why the big hurry to kill the kids?'

A Foreign Office assassin popped his head up through the skylight, and ducked down again as Doyle's shot smashed into the wood beside him. Doyle swore. He had not intended to miss.

113

Bodie said, 'Look, Ray, if I'm going to die for a meaningless cause I'd like to die with a clear hand. So cut the sleuth, okay?'

A shot came from the direction of the skylight. Bodie twisted on his haunches, let a rifle round explode towards the ducking man.

Doyle said, 'Save it.'

'Why?' snapped Bodie. 'We can't get out of here! Why drag it out?'

'To give us time to think,' Doyle retorted coolly.

'Damn thinking,' said Bodie. 'If I'm going to go, I want to go with a final blast.'

'Cowley won't let us down,' said Doyle, and ducked as bullets flew from the skylight. 'And there's only one way up here, short of a fire-ladder.'

Cowley's last card was Alex Maclean, leader of one of the most powerful unions in the country, and a personal friend of Cowley's for some years.

It was a long shot. George Cowley had remembered something about Maclean's union, and was frantically hoping that as he put two and two together he was not making five.

Maclean himself was a ragged-looking working man, in his fifties, wearing a crumpled tweed suit and smoking a wretched black briar pipe as he waited for Cowley to join him in his own car.

'Something bad, George?' he said, as Cowley sat in the passenger seat and slammed the door closed. Maclean's accent was heavily Scottish, more pronounced than Cowley's.

'Very bad, Alex,' said Cowley. He wound down the window slightly as the fumes from Maclean's pipe built up to choking proportions. 'I'm going to break every rule I ever lived by and ask you and your union committee a favour.'

Maclean's rugged features remained thoughtfully impassive as he regarded Cowley. 'I can only speak for myself, George. But you know you only have to ask.'

'Your union is one of the most powerful and militant in the country.'

'Most powerful, yes,' agreed Maclean.

'You contributed one hundred thousand pounds to the left wing resistance movement in Latin America.'

Maclean glanced at him suspiciously, then smiled thinly. 'Famine relief, George.'

Cowley laughed. 'Of course.' He hesitated a moment, then, 'What would you do, what would your union be likely to do, if they were to discover that the British Government is secretly funding the Olivares' Military Government?'

Maclean was astonished by the question. 'If that were true, you know damned well we'd pull the rug out from under the Government. We'd force an election.'

George Cowley was tense, ready to make his big request. He had to phrase the words right. For a union to take immediate, militant action, they would have to be deeply convinced that what they were doing was right.

But before Cowley could utter a word, Alex Maclean dropped his own bombshell. 'George, I have to tell you that you've been misinformed.'

Suspiciously, Cowley asked, 'In what way?'

'Our union has been involved in top secret trade agreements between the workers' revolutionary party in that country, and our own Prime Minister.'

'*What?*'

'I could be shot for telling you this, George,' Maclean puffed on his pipe. 'But there's going to be a coup in that particular country.'

'Good God.' Cowley was stunned. He stared through the windscreen, gathering his thoughts. 'Are you sure this wasn't a bluff?'

'I'm sure it wasn't,' Maclean retorted. 'There was even a General present at the meetings. One of Olivares' Chiefs of Staff, who is to lead the coup.'

'My God,' said Cowley.

'The P.M. wouldn't mess with us, George. Though some of the Cabinet, and no doubt half of Whitehall would love it.

There would be a revolution in the cabinet. It would be the end of the P.M.'s career.'

Slowly, very pointedly, Cowley said, 'Don't answer this question, Alex. Was the General in question called Alexander Molner?'

Maclean paused for a long time, not looking at Cowley. Then he said, 'I won't answer that question.'

And Cowley said, 'Thank you.'

Cowley got out of the car. Maclean glanced at him. 'How about that favour you wanted, George?'

George Cowley grinned. 'Another time, Alex. Maybe never.'

Northcott was seated behind his desk, speaking into a radiophone. 'Get it over with! And then get out as fast as possible.'

The reply came from some distance, and Cowley, listening in an outer office, didn't recognise the voice.

'Don't worry. This time we've got her.'

'Hurry!' said Northcott.

Cowley straightened up and stared at the uniformed police Superintendant and his two uniformed colleagues. Beside them stood Ministry officials, looking grim and upset. 'I think that's all we need,' Cowley said, and without waiting for a reply he turned and strode into Northcott's office.

Raoul Northcott rose from his seat, eyes bulging with shock as the small army of men advanced into the room.

Cowley walked up to him. 'Raoul Northcott. You are under arrest.'

'Arrest? What the hell for? What is this?'

Cowley said, 'You are under arrest for treason.' He reached over and picked up the radio-phone, thrusting it at Northcott, who slowly subsided back into his seat, his face a rich image of surprised confusion.

Cowley just said, 'Call them off. Now!'

And after a hesitant moment, Northcott clicked on the phone and softly spoke into the mouthpiece.

'Keep your head down lower!' Ray Doyle snapped, as a shot struck the chimney close to Diana Molner and made her wince with the sting of dust and brick in her eyes. She passed him a reloaded pistol, and Doyle turned back to the skylight and let off three rounds at the men grouped around it.

Behind them, appearing from over the edge of the roof wall, a rifleman sent two quick rounds into the chimney cluster. Bodie drove him down again with return fire.

But the situation was hopeless. They were practically out of ammunition. And there were just too many men against them.

'We've had it,' Ray Doyle said, a touch of finality in his voice.

'No!' said Diana Molner quickly. 'No. You haven't.'

She started to get up. Bodie swung round and restrained her. 'Keep still!'

'Why should all of us die?' she said loudly. 'Enough people have died for me. And it's *me* they want.'

Bodie wrenched her into a lying position. 'Stay down!'

'You don't even know what you're fighting for,' she said mockingly, and Bodie angrily silenced her with a hand to her mouth.

'This is our job, kid. You'd better believe it.'

'It's pointless!' she said, as Bodie's grip on her relaxed.

Bullets span across the chimney complex. Brick dust fell in stinging sprays across them.

And Diana wrenched herself upright, stood up and began to run towards the skylight.

'Diana!' yelled Doyle, and he made to jump after her, reaching for her, desperate to haul her back into safety.

A single shot. A rifle shot. Loud, echoing across the roof.

Diana Molner gave a grunt of shock and pain.

Her body flew backwards, across the small, defensive wall. It slumped between Bodie and Doyle, eyes staring blindly at the sky. Her mouth moved slightly, her hands seemed to scrabble at the ground.

Then she was still.

117

The blood spread out across her chest, from the narrow, fatal hole through her heart.

'Bastards!' screamed Doyle, and he rose to a standing position, holding his pistol in two hands, pumping shot after shot towards the skylight.

There was nothing – no one – to shoot at.

'Come on!' he shouted to Bodie, who knelt next to the dead girl, folding her arms across her stomach. 'The bastards are leaving! Come on ...'

'They were acting on orders,' Bodie said dully. 'Let them go.'

Doyle hesitated, watching the skylight, then his partner. After a few seconds he closed his eyes and sank down onto the wall. When he opened his eyes again he seemed dead, dulled; he stared at Diana Molner's body, and the frown that creased his forehead was less puzzlement than sadness.

Bodie said, gently, 'They probably have no more idea why she had to be killed than we have.'

'Yeah,' said Doyle. 'You're right. No more idea than we have. Or than she had herself.'

Bodie said, 'She knew what she was fighting for. They were against her. That was all she had to know.'

'Yeah,' said Doyle, climbing to his feet and walking back towards the skylight.

Epilogue

Diana Molner's body had been loaded into an ambulance. Ray Doyle watched it as it sped away between the open gates of the deserted factory. Then he turned to Bodie, gave him a sad little shrug and a smile.

Bodie punched him gently on the arm. The two of them walked over to Cowley, who had just finished talking with one of the police on the site.

Cowley said, 'I'm sorry this had to happen.'

'Me too,' said Doyle. He glanced after the ambulance. 'She was a nice kid.'

'They're all nice kids,' said Cowley. 'To start with. But Diana Molner and her brother didn't die in vain.'

'How's that, sir?' asked Bodie.

'There's been a coup in Escondia. Reports are just coming in now. General Olivares has been replaced.'

'By whom?' asked Doyle.

'By General Alexander Molner,' said Cowley. 'The girl's father.'

'So . . .' Doyle was thinking hard, his mind still numbed by the shock of the girl's death. 'So her father was behind her all the time?'

'Unlikely,' said Cowley. 'I should imagine the cocaine racket, to get money for guns, was a crackpot scheme of their own. They hatched it up after Diana had met Philip Latimer, the chemist.'

'Crackpot,' Doyle repeated. 'Yet it might have worked.'

'Except for Northcott,' said Bodie.

George Cowley nodded soberly. 'Raoul Northcott's intervention may well have forced General Molner to play his hand.'

'Apart from perverting our foreign policy,' Doyle said bitterly, 'What was Northcott getting out of it?'

119

Cowley shrugged. 'It's a little bit early to say.'

Bodie suggested, 'A china pig in Switzerland, with a slot in its back?'

'We'll find out.'

Cowley turned from them, walking towards his car.

Doyle called after him. 'Sir? Just one more thing.'

'Two things,' corrected Bodie.

'His job,' Doyle explained. 'And mine ...'

Cowley grinned, reached in through the front window of his car and picked up his R/T. 'Alpha One to Control. Operation Susie is closed, as of now. Agents Three-seven and Four-five are fully reinstated as CI5 operatives.'

He climbed into his car and drove away.

Ray Doyle looked at his partner. 'Did he thank us?'

Bodie grinned sourly and shrugged. 'Does he ever?'

the trade

william h. hallahan

'Puts William Hallahan up above Le Carré, Deighton and Co.'
The Bookseller

Journalist Bernie Parker didn't make a lot of sense that day. His words needed a bit of explanation. But Bernie is in no position to do that right now because he's just stopped several bullets outside a Paris metro. Bernie is dead. And no one knows what his last words mean.

The least Colin Thomas owes his late friend is a reason. As an international arms dealer scoring off the hotter edges of the cold war he has contacts. Contacts that lead him back to a ruthless and uninhibited woman and to the centre of a devastating plan to change the face of Europe – even if it means starting World War 3 – even if it means starting the countdown to doomsday . . .

ADVENTURE THRILLER   0 7221 4215 3   £1.75

CLIVE CUSSLER
NIGHT PROBE!

May 1914. Two top diplomats hurry home by sea and rail, each carrying a document of world-changing importance. Then the liner *Empress of Ireland* is sunk in a collision, and the 'Manhattan-Line' express plunges from a shattered bridge – both dragging their VIP passengers to watery oblivion. *Tragic coincidence – or conspiracy?*

Three-quarters of a century later a chance revelation re-opens the question. In the energy-starved, fear-torn 1980s, those long-lost papers could destroy whole nations – and Dirk Pitt, the man who raised the *Titanic*, confronts his biggest challenge yet. Racing against time, against the hired killers of enemies and allies alike – and the horrors of the sea bed – he launches his revolutionary deep-sea search craft in the hunt for the documents. 'Night Probe' has begun . . .

ADVENTURE/THRILLER   0 7221 2746 4   £1.95

TRAVERSE OF THE GODS

by Bob Langley

The Eiger, 1944 – In a desperate attempt to turn defeat into victory, German and American mountaineers are locked in an appalling struggle on the notorious North Wall of Europe's deadliest mountain – a struggle with vital implications for the development of the atomic bomb.

'Brilliant . . . in a class by itself'
Jack Higgins

'Written in the best adventure tradition'
Publishers Weekly

ADVENTURE/THRILLER   0 7221 5410 0   £1.50

And don't miss Bob Langley's other exciting thrillers:
DEATH STALK
WAR OF THE RUNNING FOX
WARLORDS
– also available in Sphere Books